Seeing you at your typewriter
inspired me to become a writer.
This is for you, Dad.
—M. Y.

SIMON SPOTLIGHT
An imprint of Simon & Schuster Children's Publishing Division
1230 Avenue of the Americas, New York, New York 10020
This Simon Spotlight hardcover edition August 2019
© 2019 by The Jim Henson Company
All rights reserved, including the right of reproduction in whole or in part in any form.
SIMON SPOTLIGHT and colophon are registered trademarks of Simon & Schuster, Inc.
For information about special discounts for bulk purchases, please contact Simon & Schuster
Special Sales at 1-866-506-1949 or business@simonandschuster.com.
Manufactured in the United States of America 0719 FFG
10 9 8 7 6 5 4 3 2 1
ISBN 978-1-4814-9131-0 (hc)
ISBN 978-1-4814-9130-3 (pbk)
ISBN 978-1-4814-9132-7 (eBook)

Jim Henson's™

FRANKEN-SCI HIGH

WHAT'S THE MATTER WITH NEWTON?

SPLAT

The boy slowly opened his eyes and sat up. He blinked under the glare of the fluorescent lights above. As his eyes focused, he could see that he was in a room filled with rows of shelves holding glass jars. Inside each jar was a mass of gelatinous gunk.

Brains.

He had no idea who he was, or where he was. He looked down at himself.

He was sort of tall—teenage-size, he guessed. He was wearing jeans that looked new. Gray sneakers. Light-blue shirt with a collar. Tagged to the shirt was a student ID: NEWTON WARP, FRESHMAN, FRANKEN-SCI HIGH.

Newton Warp. That was his name, he suddenly realized. At least he knew that. The other stuff, he wasn't so sure of. *Have I ever heard of Franken-Sci High before?* he wondered. *Nope, don't think so!*

Then he felt a prickling sensation on his neck and

turned to see that one of the brains with eyeballs attached to it was staring at him.

"What are you looking at?" Newton whispered to the brain. Then a loud voice made him jump.

"Theremin, you can't do that! That's cheating!"

Newton peeked through the shelf of brains behind him and saw two people in the next aisle. One of them was a girl. *Good, I know what a girl is!* he thought.

This girl had brown hair and big glasses. She was wearing leggings with polka dots, a fake-fur poncho, and a long scarf around her neck—or was it a snake?

And that other person is a robot, Newton thought. The robot was shorter than the girl, with a metal body, and round, blue lights where a human's eyes would go. Instead of walking, he hovered a few inches above the floor.

Newton saw that the robot was connected to one of the brain jars by a cord. One end of the cord was attached to a port on the jar, and the other was plugged into the robot's head.

"It is *not* cheating, Shelly!" the robot replied. "You would do it too if you had a plug in your head!"

"I absolutely would not, Theremin, and you know it," Shelly replied.

The robot's eyes flashed red. "Fine!" he yelled. Then he angrily pulled out the plug, disconnecting himself.

In a flash, the jar tipped over, the lid popped off, and the brain flew out and hit the window behind them. *Splat!* Newton watched, fascinated, as the brain slowly slid down the glass, leaving a trail of slime and making a loud squeaking sound before finally hitting the floor.

The robot stared at it for a moment.

The girl laughed. "It's not going to bite. Come on, let's pick it up," she said.

The robot gingerly held out the jar as the girl picked up the slimy brain, plopped it back in, and wiped her hands on her poncho as if she did this all the time.

"Whose was it?" she asked as Theremin put the jar back on the shelf.

"Sir Isaac Newton," the robot replied.

Newton? That's my name! Newton thought as he quietly watched from behind the shelves.

Then Shelly started to laugh.

"What's so funny, Shelly?" Theremin asked.

Yes, what's so funny? Newton wondered.

"Don't you get it?" she asked.

Theremin shook his head. "Get what?"

"What goes up, must come down . . . ," Shelly hinted.

Theremin shrugged.

Shelly sighed. "It's fitting because the brain slid down the window, observing the laws of gravity discovered by its former owner, Sir Isaac Newton!"

After hearing his name again, Newton felt like he had to say something.

"Newton! That's my name too!" he blurted out.

Shelly and Theremin rushed over to Newton.

"Who are you, and what are you doing here?" Theremin blurted out aggressively.

Shelly quickly stepped between him and Newton. "Sorry about that. My friend is not great with strangers," she apologized. "So let's try that again. Hi, Newton! Are you new here?"

4

"Actually, I'm not sure where 'here' is," Newton replied. "Or why I'm here, or where I came from."

"No idea at all?" Shelly asked.

"Nope."

Shelly and Theremin exchanged glances.

"Have you ever seen him on campus before?" Shelly asked Theremin.

Theremin's eyes flashed as he checked his memory banks. "Never."

"So he's new, but he doesn't know where he is, or where he came from . . ." Shelly's voice trailed off as she pondered this. "Wasn't Odifin working on an amnesia formula? Maybe Newton's a new student, and Odifin decided to test out the formula on him?"

"What's an Odifin?" Newton asked.

"Odifin Pinkwad is one of the students here at the school," Shelly replied. "But not one of the nicest."

"That's for sure," Theremin agreed.

Shelly held out her hand. "We'll help you, Newton. I'm Shelly Ravenholt, and this is Theremin Rozika."

Theremin slapped her hand away. "Wait, Shelly! We don't know where he's been."

As Theremin floated up to Newton, a flashlight popped out of a compartment on his head, and he shone it in Newton's eyes.

5

"Hey, what are you—" Newton started to protest, but the robot interrupted him.

"This won't take long," Theremin said. "We have to examine you to make sure you're not dangerous."

"I don't feel dangerous," Newton said.

"Arms up and shoes off, please," Theremin said.

Shelly tried to explain. "Don't mind Theremin. He's just being cautious. Last month Tabitha Talos made a mecho-humanoid android of herself to take tests for her. But the android wasn't properly wired and it melted."

Newton's eyes got wide, and Shelly shrugged. "Stuff like that happens all the time here."

"And 'here' is . . . ?" Newton asked.

"Right," Shelly said. "Sorry. You're in Franken-Sci High. It's a school for kids who want to be scientists. Most of us are the children of scientists, but not all of us."

"*Mad* scientists," Theremin grumbled. He got to work even though Newton had only taken off one shoe.

"What's a mad scientist?" Newton asked.

"It depends on your point of view," Shelly replied. "The world might see some of our parents and ancestors as *mad* scientists, but that's just because they were not afraid to take risks! To explore areas of science that others might find frightening or unconventional. To imagine that anything—"

6

"Aha!" Theremin cried. He pointed to the bottom of Newton's foot. "A bar code."

Newton and Shelly looked. Theremin was right. The black lines of a bar code glistened on the bottom of Newton's foot.

"Now, that's interesting," Shelly remarked, adjusting her glasses to see better.

Theremin's eyes flashed, turning to red lasers as he scanned the bar code.

"Nothing," he muttered. Then he scanned it again.

"So, if many of you are the kids of scientists, does that mean I am too?" Newton asked.

"You could be," Shelly replied. "Are you sure you don't remember?"

Newton shook his head. "I'm not even sure if I have a family."

"Oh, how awful!" Shelly said sympathetically. "Listen, I'm thinking that Odifin must have used an amnesia formula on you. He might have thought it would be funny to prank the new kid."

"That sounds like the most logical explanation," Theremin agreed, and then he tried reading the bar code again. "Still nothing."

"Theremin and I can take you to the school's headmistress," Shelly continued. "She'll make Odifin give you the antidote. She'll know who your family is too."

The bar code . . . amnesia formula . . . mad scientists . . . Newton's head was spinning. *How do I know this girl and this robot are telling me the truth?* he wondered. For some reason, he felt he could trust Shelly. Besides, he

had no choice. He had no one else to trust right now.

"I'd love to go see her," Newton replied. "Except . . ." He looked over at Theremin.

Theremin was still holding on to Newton's foot. His eyes kept flashing . . . and flashing . . . and flashing. . . .

"Uh-oh!" Shelly said. "Theremin, are you glitching?"

Theremin whacked the side of his metal head with his hand. "I'm fine," he insisted. "It's probably just a loose wire." He whacked his head again, and his red eyes flashed . . . and flashed. His head bopped up and down.

"It doesn't make sense!" Theremin cried, filled with frustration. "It's a simple bar code. Why can't I scan it?"

"Let me help," Shelly said, and she pressed a reset button on the back of his head.

Theremin's eyes stopping flashing. His head stopped bopping.

"Better?" Shelly asked.

"I think I need to get my eyes checked," Theremin responded. "My bar code scanner must not be working."

"First we have to help Newton," Shelly said.

"*You* can bring him to Mumtaz," Theremin snapped. "I need to see Nurse Bunsen."

"All right. I'll check in with you later, okay?" Shelly said, but Theremin floated away without another word.

Newton put his shoe back on. "So, this brain room is

part of the school?" he asked.

"It's part of the library, actually," Shelly explained as they walked. "Many of the world's greatest scientists donated their brains to the school. We can connect with them to research a project, or to study for a test."

"So why did you say that Theremin was cheating?" Newton asked.

She showed him a rectangular device. "Everyone has a tablet—it's like a small computer. You'll probably remember that when you get your memory back. You can plug it into a port on the jar of the brain you want to get information from. The brain gives out electrical impulses that communicate with the tablet."

Newton nodded like he understood, although he really didn't.

"Theremin has a tablet too," Shelly continued, "but he was plugging the brain directly into his own hard drive. That's against the rules."

"I hope Isaac Newton's brain is all right," he added.

"Me too," Shelly said.

As they made their way to the headmistress's office, Newton was silent. Students walked by, talking and laughing, and Newton looked at every face, hoping to find a familiar one. But he didn't recognize a soul.

CHAPTER 2

What's Your Major Malfunction?

Theremin floated through the halls of Franken-Sci High toward the Student Clinic. He was nervous. He'd never had to visit Nurse Bunsen before, but he had seen other freshmen students come back from the clinic looking pale and unsteady. When he'd asked them what had happened, they would usually mumble something about "unusual methods," but they couldn't complain too much because they'd been cured.

Not being able to perform a simple bar code scan had shaken up Theremin. That had never happened before.

It is Father's fault, Theremin mused. *He gave me human emotions and thoughts but only "adequate" intelligence.*

Theremin knew that his father's greatest fear was that Theremin would be even smarter than he was. So Dr. Rozika had worked a flaw into Theremin's programming. If Theremin began to do really well at one thing, he'd immediately lose his ability to do something else.

But I wasn't doing anything great before my scanner conked out, Theremin remembered. *In fact, I had just messed up, sending that brain flying. . . .*

At least Shelly didn't mind that he was a bit different. She'd always understood him. When his dad had first enrolled him in Franken-Sci High, the other robot students had been friendly toward him. But then he'd started glitching . . . and because he had human-like emotions, glitching made him feel really angry.

One day he'd failed a simple quiz in Engineering Artificial Life Forms, and at lunch Klaatu had teased him about it.

"How could you fail at that, dude?" his robot friend had asked. "I mean, you *are* an artificial life form!"

Theremin had gotten angry and smashed everyone's algae-infused pudding cups, and even though robots don't need to eat for fuel, some of them had taste receptors and had gotten really bummed. Theremin wasn't allowed to eat lunch with them anymore.

The next day Theremin had been sulking at a table by himself when Shelly walked up.

"Can I sit here?" she asked, with her big smile, and of course Theremin had said yes. And the two had been best friends ever since.

And now here is this Newton guy, appearing out of

nowhere, Theremin thought. *Shelly had been all smiley and friendly with him, too. What did that mean?*

He stepped up to the door to the Student Clinic, and the door slid up into the ceiling. Theremin scanned the room. Inside, two kids were sitting on a bench. Across from the bench was an empty desk with a grinning skull on top, along with a plaque that read: NURSE CARLOTTA BUNSEN.

On the wall in front of Theremin was another door decorated with instructive posters. They said things like: SAFETY GOGGLES SAVE EYES! and BE CAREFUL WORKING WITH ELECTRICITY: IT CAN BE SHOCKING!

Theremin sat down on the bench next to a kid he knew, Gustav Goddard. Gustav turned to Theremin.

"What are you here for?" he asked.

"Code-scanning problem," Theremin replied. "You?"

Gustav wiggled his eyebrows—or rather, the part of his face where his eyebrows should have been.

"Had a little problem in my Unconventional Chemistry class," Gustav replied. "I sort of blew my eyebrows off."

"I didn't even notice," Theremin replied. He nodded toward the girl sitting on Gustav's other side. Her hands were curled up into little balls and she was licking them.

"What's up with her?" Theremin asked.

"Oh, that's Tori Twitcher," Gustav said. "She got hit by a mind-control ray by accident and now she thinks she's a cat."

Tori looked at Theremin. *"Meow!"*

The door with the posters on it opened, and a boy walked out. He had a patch over his right eye.

Nurse Bunsen stepped out behind him.

"Run along now, Leopold," she said. "Don't worry,

it should grow back by tomorrow. Or maybe Tuesday. Wednesday, at the latest."

Theremin studied her. She wore a spacesuit instead of a nurse's uniform. A clear helmet. Short hair that had little swirls in it like soft-serve ice cream.

"You're next, Tori," she said.

Tori was swatting at a fly. She didn't look up.

"Here, kitty kitty," Nurse Bunsen said in a sweet voice. Tori's head jerked up, and then on all fours she followed the nurse into the exam room.

"I'm glad all that's wrong with me is some missing eyebrows," Gustav remarked.

"Uh-huh," Theremin said. He wasn't really listening. He was still thinking about that new guy. Newton was definitely human, not mecho-humanoid, so they didn't have to worry about him exploding. *But there is still something weird about that guy,* Theremin thought.

He hoped that Shelly's theory would turn out to be right: that Newton was the victim of an amnesia formula, a simple prank, and that Mumtaz would fix it. Then Newton would remember that he had other friends, and he could go hang out with *them.* And Shelly and Theremin could go back to being best buddies again. A terrific twosome. A dynamite duo . . .

The door creaked open again. "Good as new, Tori,"

Nurse Bunsen said as Tori exited, looking normal again. "Gustav, you're next."

Tori looked at Theremin and Gustav. "I hate Mondays," she said.

Gustav went into the exam room, and Theremin's robot brain tracked the time as he was waiting. Exactly 17.4 seconds later, Gustav came back out. Where his eyebrows should have been, two new eyebrows had been drawn on in marker. Purple marker.

"Whaddya think?" Gustav asked, wiggling his marker eyebrows.

Theremin thought Gustav looked ridiculous, even for a human, but he didn't want to say that with Nurse Bunsen standing right there.

"Um, fab," Theremin replied, searching his memory banks for synonyms. "Cool. Brilliant."

"Thanks!" Gustav said brightly, and left.

Nurse Bunsen crooked a finger at Theremin. "Come on in, Mr. Rozika."

Theremin cautiously followed her into the next room. His danger sensors started to jump a little. In the back of the room was a huge aquarium filled with electric eels. They sizzled in the water.

"What seems to be the trouble, Theremin?" Nurse Bunsen asked.

"Something's wrong with my bar code scanner," he replied.

"Is that all?" Nurse Bunsen sounded disappointed. "Let's give you a little test."

She pressed a button in the wall and part of the wall opened up. A metal tray slid out, stacked with a group of items in a pyramid shape.

"When your father founded the robotics lab here, he designed this robot vision test," she explained. "Start scanning the items on the bottom, and move to the top."

Theremin floated over to the items. The first item on the bottom left was a package of toilet paper. Theremin's eyes flashed red over the bar code.

"Eight-count of Super Soft Stuff, double-ply," he reported, and Nurse Bunsen nodded.

He moved to the next item—a jar full of eyeballs. Theremin scanned the bar code.

"Twenty-four assorted replacement eyeballs," the robot announced.

"Keep going, Theremin," the nurse encouraged him.

He scanned his way up the pyramid.

"One gravity-resistant soccer ball."

"One loaf of gluten-free bread."

"Microscope, Curie model 620."

Nurse Bunsen put a hand up to stop him. "Your

scanner is working fine, Theremin. Better than fine," she told him, and then she laughed. "You know, they always need good scanning equipment in the cafeteria, if you're looking for a part-time job."

Then she cackled at her own joke.

Scanning equipment.

His processors started to overheat. *I am no mere piece of equipment,* he thought. *I am a boy—yes, a robot boy, but a boy! With thoughts and feelings. And right now I am feeling . . .*

"*Aaaaaaaaaaaaah!*" Theremin screamed. He knocked down the pyramid, sending everything crashing to the floor. The jar of eyeballs broke, and the eyeballs rolled all over the room.

"And it looks like your energy levels are just fine, Theremin," Nurse Bunsen said.

Couldn't she see that he was upset? That just made him angrier.

"I'm outta here!" he announced, and he burst through the door, sending shards of metal flying, shredding the "Safety Goggles Save Eyes" poster in the process, and leaving a Theremin-shaped hole in the door. Theremin didn't even notice.

Everything is going wrong! he fumed. *And it all started with the new kid!*

CHAPTER 3

The Most Annoying, Sneezy Song in the World

Newton was listening to Shelly chat away as they walked to the headmistress's office.

"The last class of the day ended about an hour ago," Shelly informed him. "Now is the time when most students do homework or extracurriculars. There are lots of after-school clubs. I can tell you all about them."

"Um, what about you?" Newton asked. "I mean, I don't know who I am, but I'd like to know who you are."

"Oh, sure," Shelly said, sounding a little surprised. "Sorry. Theremin says I can talk faster than he can process me sometimes. Anyway, my family, the Ravenholts, is a distant branch of the Frankenstein family."

Newton looked at her blankly.

"Oh, that's right, the amnesia," Shelly said. "You don't know about Frankenstein. Dr. Victor Frankenstein was a very famous mad scientist, who—"

Newton interrupted her. "I'm still not even sure what

a mad scientist is or does."

"Sorry," Shelly said. "When someone is called a mad scientist, it's because some people think the things they study are wrong or dangerous, even if they aren't."

Newton nodded. "I think I get it."

"Good. So, anyway, Victor Frankenstein created a creature that some people thought was a monster," Shelly went on. "It's sort of his claim to fame. There were books and movies written about him and everything. People don't think he was real, but he was, and he was one of the founders of this school."

"Do *you* make monsters too?" Newton asked her.

"I guess it depends on your definition of 'monster,'" Shelly replied. "I really like animals, so I've been working on ways to protect defenseless ones by making hybrids."

She held up her tablet and scrolled to a picture. "That's a Chihuahua. They're tiny little dogs. So I bio-designed this one with camouflage fur, for protection."

Newton nodded. "So it can blend in its fur with its surroundings."

"Exactly," Shelly said. "Animals are my thing, I guess. So my goal is to find ways to use science to help them."

They passed a glass case filled with trophies, each one flashing holographic images of the student who had won them. Newton caught his reflection in the glass, and stopped.

It's my face! he thought. *I'm seeing it for the first time. Or am I?*

The face looked kind of familiar. Small nose. Big eyes. Dark, wavy hair with a white streak running through it. And was that a faint tint of blue in his skin? Or was that just an effect of the bright light overhead?

He glanced around at the other students. Some were short, some were tall. Some had crazy-colored hair. Some were made of metal, polymers, and plastic, like Theremin. He didn't look any stranger than any of them.

So why do I feel so different?

"Newton?" Shelly called back to him, and then she stopped. "Oh, the trophies. It's a very competitive school. In fact, the Mad Science Fair is coming up soon. Whoever wins will get a trophy that will go in this case."

"Oh cool," Newton said, snapping back to attention.

They walked a little farther and stopped in front of a door with a glass window etched with HEADMISTRESS MOBIUS MUMTAZ.

"We're here," Shelly told him. As she reached for the doorknob, a girl with blond hair bumped into her.

"Did the *perfect* Shelly Ravenholt get into trouble?" the girl asked.

"I'm not in trouble, Mimi," Shelly answered her. "Newton here is new, and I'm bringing him to see Ms. Mumtaz."

Mimi faced Newton. "New student, huh? What's your whole name?"

"Um, Newton Warp," Newton replied. Something about this girl was making him feel uneasy.

"Where are you from, Newton Warp?" Mimi asked.

"Mimi, can you please save the questions for later?" Shelly asked with a sigh. "Newton's having kind of a weird day."

Mimi smiled sweetly. "Sure, Shelly," she said. Then she pulled a makeup compact out of her purse and opened it. "I'll just stop questioning Newton and fix my face. The lighting in these halls can make your nose look so shiny. Am I right, Shelly?"

Mimi picked up the powder puff and blew on it, causing powder to fly out and hit Shelly's nose!

Why would Mimi do that? he wondered.

"Achoo!" Shelly sneezed. *"Achoo!"*

And then Shelly started to sing. A lot.

"This is the most annoying song in the world, the most annoying song in the world, the most annoying song in the world, and it goes like this . . ."

"Shelly?" Newton asked, but Mimi pulled him aside.

"Listen, Newton Warp," she said. "My parents warned me that there might be spies at this school. You're trying to steal my science fair project ideas, aren't you? If you're a spy, you'd better confess right now."

Mimi was the daughter of Crispina and Karl Crowninshield, the founders of Crowninshield

Industries. They made products like the World's Lumpiest Pillow and other items designed to make people miserable . . . but Newton didn't know that yet.

"*This is the most annoying song in the world . . . ,*" Shelly sang.

Newton looked over at Shelly, then back at Mimi. "I'm not a spy," he answered cautiously. "At least, I don't think I am."

Mimi's blue eyes narrowed. "What does that mean?"

"It means, I can't remember anything about myself," Newton answered honestly.

Mimi frowned. "You like to play games, huh? Well, I can play games too."

"*Achoo! Achoo! Achoo!*" Shelly sneezed.

Mimi poked a finger in Newton's chest. "Listen, 'New-ton'—"

Before she could finish her threat, the office door opened, and the headmistress stepped out.

"What on earth is going on out here?" she asked.

"*Achoo!*" Shelly sneezed, took a breath, and then kept on singing. "*This is the most annoying song in the world . . .*"

Mimi started to slip away, but Mumtaz stopped her.

"Mimi, what did you do?" the headmistress asked.

"It was an accident," Mimi said. "Somehow, I put

purolated hydrobvious into my compact by mistake, and . . ."

Shaking her head, Mumtaz snorted and muttered, "Hmph, it activates the brain's misery center." She then pulled a small vial out of her pocket, unscrewed the top, and held it under Shelly's nose. "Breathe," Mumtaz instructed.

Shelly obeyed. "*Ah—*" The sneeze stopped midway. "Thank you!"

The headmistress turned to Mimi and shook her head. "Can't you behave yourself for even five minutes, Mimi?" she asked. "You were just in my office, promising me you would stay out of trouble, and yet . . . here we are."

"It was an accident," Mimi insisted.

Mumtaz sighed. "You are not getting off the hook this time," she said. "Go to detention. Now!" Then she suddenly noticed Newton and her expression softened.

"Shelly, are you with this boy?" she asked, and Shelly nodded.

Mimi headed to detention as Mumtaz said, "You two, follow me."

Newton and Shelly followed Mumtaz inside her office. Newton found himself slightly mesmerized by the headmistress's colorful outfit: orange and yellow tights, black shiny boots, a black necklace, and a dark

green dress with pink arm warmers.

And Mumtaz's hair was just as colorful, a short bob streaked with orange and purple strands. Her large eyeglasses had thick dark frames. Her thin face reminded him of a . . . a bird.

The headmistress sat behind her desk. When Newton saw Shelly sit in a chair in front of the desk, Newton took her cue and sat down next to her.

"Now, then, let's—" Mumtaz began, but she was interrupted by a ringing sound. The lenses in her eyeglasses flickered, then brightened, and then transformed into translucent screens. Words began scrolling on the screens.

"Sorry, it appears there's a slight emergency," she said as she read the screens. "Professor Yuptuka decided to treat her students to a lovely French snack and teleported them to Paris. But she miscalculated the coordinates, and they've landed on top of the Eiffel Tower. Unfortunately, Yuptuka is very afraid of heights."

Mumtaz blinked and started speaking again. "Professor, you know that teleportation must be approved through official channels. You should have filled out a form."

There was silence as Mumtaz read the response. "Yes, I know that doesn't help your problem right now. Why don't you try teleporting to a location on the ground? Of course you didn't think of that. Good luck, then. *Au revoir!*"

The glasses flickered again and returned to normal.

"Now then," she said. "What's brought you two to my office?"

"Theremin and I found Newton in the library," Shelly replied. "He doesn't know who he is or where he's from."

"Hmm," Headmistress Mumtaz said, eyeing Newton.

"I heard that Odifin Pinkwad was working on an amnesia formula," Shelly went on. "So I was thinking that maybe since Newton is a new student, Odifin played a prank on him."

"That's possible," Mumtaz replied. "Newton, is it? Let's get you settled in. May I see your ID please?"

Newton unpinned the ID and handed it to her. Mumtaz took it from him and then swiped the air in front of her. A holographic screen popped up.

"I'll just run this through the student database," she said.

Mumtaz swiped the ID on the side of the screen. The back of the screen facing Shelly and Newton was mostly hidden by green laser lines, so they couldn't tell what she was reading. Newton noticed the headmistress

flinch and then inch closer to the screen.

"Is something wrong?" Newton asked.

Mumtaz's face quickly reverted to a blank expression. "Nothing unusual. Just that you're registered as Newton Warp, and you're allergic to flamingoes."

"What are flamingoes?" Newton asked.

"We're in the beginning of our first semester here at Franken-Sci High, so I'll assume you transferred from another school," she said. "I see you're already enrolled in a few freshman classes, but you'll have to select some electives in the next few days to get a full schedule. Let me get a tablet for you."

Mumtaz got up and walked over to a supply closet.

Newton leaned toward Shelly.

"She doesn't seem very surprised that I turned up in the library with no memory," he whispered.

"She's not easily flustered," Shelly responded. "As cool as water mixed with frozen cucumber extract. You'd have to be, to be in charge of this school. Weird things happen every day."

Newton nodded and glanced around the room. Portraits of women with birdlike faces and thick dark glasses adorned the walls.

Mumtaz returned and handed Newton a tablet and a black drawstring bag filled with Franken-Sci High spirit wear.

"Those are the former headmistresses of Franken-Sci High," she said, smiling at the portraits. "Each one a Mumtaz. Now, here you go. You're all set for classes."

Newton stared down at the tablet and the bag for a minute. Then he looked back up.

"Is this it? What about my memory? Does the database say anything about my family? Or who I am?" he asked.

Mumtaz looked at the screen again, squinting. "No, there's nothing here," she said.

A wave of disappointment swept over Newton.

Mumtaz swiped the air and the holographic screen disappeared. Then she walked around the desk and put a hand on Newton's shoulder.

"But you're enrolled in the school, and your tuition is paid for, so I know you're supposed to be here," she said. "Maybe there's a glitch in the system that's masking the information about your family. I'll look into it."

"And you'll question Odifin?" Shelly asked.

"Certainly," Mumtaz replied. "In the meantime, I suggest that you make yourself at home here. I'm sure you'll find, Newton, that Franken-Sci High is like one big, happy family."

"One big, happy family," Newton repeated.

"I'm assigning you to dorm room YTH-125," she

told him. "It's all in your tablet. Your locker number's in there too. Shelly, since you two are already friends, would you mind showing Newton the ropes? Oh, and teach him how to use the portal to the campus. He'll have to pass the portal test in a few weeks, just like everyone else."

"Sure," Shelly said brightly. "We can start right away."

Shelly stood up, and Newton followed her lead. Mumtaz held out her hand. Newton guessed he was supposed to do the same, and Mumtaz shook it.

"Feel free to stop by anytime, Newton, to let me know how you're doing," she said.

"Okay, thanks," Newton said.

Something told him that Headmistress Mumtaz was not telling him the whole truth. It made him even more determined to find out what was really going on.

CHAPTER 4

Today's Secret Flavor Is . . . Cotton Candy!

When they left Mumtaz's office, Shelly could see that Newton was worried.

"It's going to be okay, Newton, I promise," she told him. "But I'm sorry if I made it seem like Mumtaz could fix everything. I didn't mean to get your hopes up. Honestly, I'm a little confused."

Newton hesitated. "Did you—did you get the feeling she's, maybe, hiding something?"

Shelly nodded. "Whatever it is, I am going to do everything I can to figure it out, okay?"

Newton looked at her with sad eyes. He had reminded her of a lost puppy dog from the moment she saw him, and she was a sucker for any animal that needed help, or was hurt or lost.

Back home it seemed like they were drawn to her. It was some kind of strange sixth sense. She once caught a baby bird just as it fell out of its nest. An injured

squirrel showed up on her doorstep, and she made a bionic leg for it. She even knitted a bodysuit for a bald porcupine, and nursed a star-nosed mole with a hurt paw back to health. Shelly felt very lucky that her mom and dad appreciated what she was doing and let her turn the garage into a wildlife rescue center.

As Shelly got more interested in mad science, she started making animal hybrids. Some people called them "monsters," but Shelly's goal was for the greater good. She wanted to make animals that could withstand harsh conditions, repair their own bones, and survive oil spills. Animal rescue was her first love, and she was grateful that when she had left for Franken-Sci High, her parents promised to keep her rescue work going.

When she thought of Newton, who had no idea who his family was, she felt a pang of sympathy. She wanted to help him.

"Let's go to your locker first," Shelly told him. "Let me see your tablet."

Newton passed it to her, and Shelly nodded.

"We're in the same locker hive," she said, handing the tablet back to him. "Come on! To get to our lockers, you make a right here at the Sentient Vegetation Incubator," she said, pointing to a glass wall where Newton could see that some unfortunate student was wrestling with an aggressive ivy vine. "Try to remember that if you get lost."

"Well, my brain is pretty empty right now, so I should be able to fill it with a lot more stuff," Newton joked.

Shelly laughed. "That's pretty funny, Newton! Guess your brain bank *is* pretty empty."

She made a right turn and about halfway down the hall, stopped in front of a gleaming metal locker.

"Locker number 352.17," she said. "You're lucky you're on the first hive level."

Shelly looked up, and Newton saw that rows and rows of lockers, going up as high as fifty feet, were stacked on top of one another. "I'm all the way up there," she told him.

Then she looked back at Newton's locker. "They're a bit tricky to open. I'll show you," she said.

She pointed to a glass pad on the right side of the locker door.

"Students here are very protective of their experiments and their research, so the school developed a triple-factor verification program for lockers," she explained. "First, it reads your fingerprint."

She motioned for Newton to touch a button on the pad with his finger. He obeyed, and a *beep* sounded.

"Next is the eye scan," Shelly said. "Just open your

eyes wide and put them close to the pad. They don't have to touch."

Newton leaned forward. A green light flashed across his eyes. *Beep!*

"So far, so good," Shelly said. "Finally, the saliva analysis. You need to lick the lines on the bottom of the pad, and it recognizes your DNA. Professor Phlegm is in charge of it, and he chooses a different flavor for the pad every day. What kind of flavor we get usually depends on his mood. He must be in a good mood today because it tastes like cotton candy."

"Cotton candy tastes good?" Newton asked.

"Try it and see," Shelly said.

Newton cautiously leaned down again and licked the pad. Then he smiled.

"Good," Newton agreed, nodding.

"I'm glad," Shelly said. "Yesterday it tasted like a sweaty exercise mat!"

Newton moved to open the door, and Shelly put her arm in front of him.

"Stop!" she cried. "Do it slowly, and look first before you reach in. There have been black holes popping up inside some of the lockers recently. The Physics Club has been trying to get them under control, but black holes are, well, kind of major. They'll suck you into—oblivion!"

"That doesn't sound good," Newton said.

"It's not," Shelly said.

Newton slowly opened the door and peered in.

"All clear," Shelly said. "When you get books and stuff, you can stash them in here between classes. Or use your locker to store anything you want to keep safe. At least now you know how to open it."

Newton closed the door, and Shelly heard his stomach growl loudly. She giggled.

"Sounds like you're hungry." she said.

"Hungry?" Newton repeated.

"It's when your stomach feels empty, and you want to eat food," Shelly said.

Newton nodded. "Then I guess I'm hungry."

"Come on, let's go to the cafeteria," she said. "They should still be serving food."

Shelly led him down the hallway to a large glass tube. She pressed a button and the tube hissed open. She stepped inside and Newton followed.

"You just have to say or think where you want to go, or press a button on the screen, and the tube will take you there," Shelly explained. "It's a little intense the first few times you try it."

"Intense? I woke up in a room full of brains and I don't know who I am," Newton said. "Bring it on!"

Shelly paused, then giggled again. "Fourth floor, please," she said, and she and Newton gasped as they got sucked up the tube. They came to a stop a few seconds later, and a door opened up. Newton put his hand on Shelly's shoulder to steady himself.

Shelly pointed to their reflection in the glass. Their hair was sticking out all over the place!

"We call it the Albert Einstein Effect," Shelly told him. "Quick pat down, and we're good to go," she added, smoothing down her hair with the palms of her hands.

Newton did the same, and then they stepped out into a noisy, crowded cafeteria filled with students sitting at tables. Strange smells filled the air, and Shelly heard Newton's stomach growl again.

"It's pretty crowded, and we've got a lot to cover," she said. "Come on, let's use the food-erators."

Shelly headed through the crowd and stopped a few seconds later when she bumped into Theremin, holding a tray of food.

"You're late," he said stiffly. He looked about as wooden as a robot could look, given that he was mostly metal.

"Sorry, it took a while in Ms. Mumtaz's office, and I've got to show Newton around," Shelly said. "Hey, how did it go with Nurse Bunsen?"

"My scanners are fine," Theremin replied. "So that thing

on Newton's foot can't be a bar code. It must be a tattoo or something."

Newton slapped his forehead. "The bar code! I meant to ask the headmistress about that, but I forgot."

Shelly shook her head. "That doesn't make sense. Kids don't usually get tattooed!"

"Maybe wherever he comes from, everyone gets tattooed," Theremin said, and his voice was cranky. "How should I know? I'm just a stupid robot."

"You know I don't like it when you use that word, Theremin," Shelly said, ignoring his crankiness as always. "Glad you're okay."

"So you're not eating with me, then?" Theremin asked.

"We can't," Shelly replied.

"I wasn't offering to eat with *him*," Theremin said. His eyes flashed green.

Shelly knew that meant he was jealous, but she also knew she wouldn't be able to get through to him until he cooled off. "Catch you later!" she said, trying to sound breezy in hopes that he would lighten up. "Newton and I need to eat fast so I can give him a tour of the campus!"

They got moving again, and Shelly stopped in front of some tall machines with glass fronts. Through the glass, Newton could see various items vacuum-packed in silver-colored foil.

"My treat today, since you're new," Shelly said, producing her ID card from under her poncho. "Let's see, what looks good? How about a bean burrito?"

"Sure! I don't know what that is, but it sounds good," Newton replied.

Shelly swiped her card, pressed some buttons, and a tray emerged with two foil-wrapped burritos on it.

"Here you go, Newton," she said, handing one to him. "There's a free table over there," Shelly said. "We can scarf these down, and then I'll give you the rest of the tour."

They sat down at a table. Newton popped the entire burrito into his mouth, foil and all, and began to chew.

"This is um, . . . interesting," he remarked.

Shelly looked at him, wide-eyed.

"You know you're supposed to unwrap that, right?" she asked. "Or maybe you don't?" She unwrapped her burrito to demonstrate.

"Okay, if you say so . . . ," Newton said, then spit out a ball of foil into his hand. He took a bite of the burrito, this time without foil. "It does taste much better this way. Thanks!"

"Sure," Shelly said, and then leaned closer to him. "So, Newton, I was wondering. What exactly do you remember? I mean, you talk—you know *words* and

all—so you must remember some things, right?"

"It's weird," Newton replied. "Like, some things I just know. I know that this is a table and that's a wall and that's a door. When I met you, I thought you were friendly and I knew what that meant."

Shelly smiled.

"But other things, I just don't know," Newton went on. "Like how I didn't know what a mad scientist was. Or a flamingo." He shrugged.

"I'm sure Mumtaz will figure this out," Shelly said. Then her eyes lit up. "Hey, what if you're walking around in an encephalo-magnetic dream state? Maybe you'll wake up tomorrow and remember everything."

"I sure hope so," Newton said.

Shelly wiped her hands on a napkin and then produced a colorful piece of folded paper from under her poncho. It had a picture of a building on the front and the words FRANKEN-SCI HIGH in big letters. Underneath was the symbol of a brain and a motto: A BRAIN IS A TERRIBLE THING TO WASTE . . . UNLESS YOU CAN GROW ANOTHER ONE.

"This is the school brochure," she said. "It's, like, a little book that tells you about the school and what we learn here. But it's also a portal. When you're outside the school and you need to get here, you just fold

the brochure in a specific way and a Euclidean vortex will open."

Shelly demonstrated. She opened the brochure once, and then twice, so that it was now shaped like a big square. Newton watched as she folded in each corner of the square. And then she made some more folds. It looked kind of confusing.

"Then you just fold it in half one more time, and the portal opens," Shelly said. She unfolded the brochure and passed it to Newton. "Here, you try."

He took the brochure from her. He folded down the left corner. Then the right corner. Shelly saw little beads of sweat on his forehead.

"You're getting it," she said.

Newton held up the brochure, and his fingers were stuck to the paper!

"Hmm," Shelly said. "Must be burrito grease." She handed him a napkin.

Newton took the napkin—and the napkin stuck to his fingers!

Shelly pried off the napkin and looked at it. It was grease-free.

"Hmm," she said. "Try again."

Newton touched the brochure, and it stuck to all his fingers this time. Shelly carefully pried it off.

"Don't worry about it," she said. "Let me put it in your bag for you. We can practice another time. Every freshman gets tested on portal opening, but that's not for a while yet. We have plenty of time."

She stood up. "You should read the brochure anyway. It tells you all about the school. Like, I forgot to mention where the school is located. Come on, I think it'll be easier to show you."

Shelly led Newton to an outdoor patio off the cafeteria. She pointed to the expanse outside—tropical trees as far as the eye could see, and an eerie green fog on the horizon.

"We're in the middle of the Bermuda Triangle," she explained. "It's an area in the Atlantic Ocean where people say strange things happen, and airplanes and ships apparently disappear into thin air. The truth is, that fog out there is what keeps Franken-Sci High hidden from the rest of the world."

"Whoa," Newton said. "Do kids ever go outside?"

"Sure," Shelly replied. "The dorms are out there—the buildings where we sleep. And the school store is out there, and a few places to eat. But I should finish showing you the main school building first. Let's head to the gym."

"And that is . . . ?" Newton asked.

"It's where you go to exercise your body," Shelly informed him. "It's filled with some really cool equipment. I'll show you."

Shelly led him out of the cafeteria, down a hallway, and into a large room filled with clear glass equipment and exercise cubicles. One boy was running on a glass treadmill, with a holographic projection of a giant octopus chasing him. Newton raised his eyebrows and looked at Shelly.

"Training motivation," Shelly explained.

Nearby, a girl was inside a glass box, floating in mid-air, but running at the same time.

"Hover jogging," Shelly told him. "You work out your muscles without stressing your joints."

They turned a corner and came to a room with a blue tile floor and a big, glistening rectangle of water. The room was quiet, and empty of students except for a lifeguard.

"And here's the pool," Shelly said.

Newton's eyes got wide. He tossed his drawstring bag aside and jumped right into the pool with all his clothes on!

"Newton! What are you doing?" Shelly yelled.

She peered over the edge, scanning the bottom of the pool, but couldn't see her new friend anywhere.

Shelly blinked. *It must be the fluorescent lighting playing tricks on my eyes,* she thought.

"Newton?" she called out.

There was no response. The water was still. It seemed like Newton should be coming up for air soon.

"Newton?" she called again.

She looked around. Had Newton climbed out of the pool? Was he playing a trick on her? No, she would have seen him climb out. *He must be in the water, but I just can't see him!* she reasoned.

"Newton!"

On the very bottom of the pool, the water seemed to be rippling, but she still didn't see Newton. Panic rose up within her. Had he been sucked down a drain? And why hadn't the lifeguard heard her yelling? She looked over and saw that the lifeguard was looking in the water, too, but since the pool looked empty, he wasn't moving.

Since the lifeguard wasn't responding, Shelly ran to the nearest emergency robotic lifeguard box. She pulled the lever and a siren sounded. Robotic hands emerged from the wall and reached for the pool—just as Newton came to the surface.

"What's that noise?" Newton asked.

The human lifeguard looked confused, rubbed his eyes, and then stared at Newton in shock.

"What happened to you?" Shelly yelled at Newton. "I thought you drowned or something!"

Then for a split second, Shelly thought she saw fish-like gills on Newton's neck. But the skin quickly closed up. She blinked again.

If my eyes are playing tricks on me, that's some trick! she thought.

The sirens were still blaring. The human lifeguard made sure Newton was okay, pressed a cancel button to turn off the siren, and went straight to Nurse Bunsen's office to get his eyes checked since he could have sworn no one was in the pool.

Shelly led Newton out of the pool area and stopped once they reached the hallway.

"So what happened in that pool?" she asked. "Why did you jump in?"

"I don't know," he replied with a shrug. "I guess . . . I guess I know how to swim."

"You were down there an awfully long time," Shelly said. "Weren't your lungs bursting?"

Newton shrugged again. "It felt normal to me."

Shelly frowned. She was used to weird things happening at Franken-Sci High. There were kids who looked and acted way weirder than Newton. But that was just it. Newton wasn't a robot, or a brain in a jar

like Odifin. He looked like a regular kid. But Shelly was starting to think that Newton was far, far from normal. And maybe that was a clue to who he really was. Still, she decided not to tell him until she knew more.

"Sure, normal," Shelly said, and the friendly smile returned to her face. "I think we should head to your dorm room, though. You must be tired."

And I want to do a little bit of research on what might make a human sprout gills . . . she added to herself.

CHAPTER 5

It's a Goo Thing

Newton thought that Shelly was unusually quiet as they made their way to the dorm building. He was still sopping wet, so she made him wrap one of the school's pool towels around his shoulders when she brought him outside. They walked along a path lined with tall trees with feathery leaves on top. The air smelled nice to Newton, and he guessed that the smell was coming from the flowers on the border of the path, which were brilliant shades of red and orange.

Newton followed Shelly to a tall brick building. Inside was another glass transport tube. Shelly and Newton entered.

"Freshman Floor," Shelly said, and *whoosh!* They quickly shot up four floors. "This is the boys' dorm," she said, smoothing her hair as they stepped out into a hallway. Newton saw that and patted down his hair too, which was a bit drier after the ride.

"Your room—and your roommate—should be right down here." Shelly said. She walked a bit and stopped in front of a door marked YTH-125. "I'll meet you here at seven a.m. tomorrow. We'll grab some breakfast, and then I'll take you to the classes on your schedule, and some of mine in case you like them. Okay?"

"Okay," Newton replied. He glanced at the closed door behind him. "So, do you want to meet my room—"

"Things to do!" Shelly said quickly, and dashed off down the hallway, trying to act like nothing was out of the ordinary.

Newton shrugged.

Then he stared at the closed door. Beyond it was his room—his new home. He took a deep breath and knocked before opening the door.

"Hello there! You must be my new roomie!"

Newton stopped in his tracks and stared at the kid in front of him. Even though Newton had lost almost all his memory, he was pretty sure he had never seen a kid like this before.

His roommate wore a heavy coat, rubber gloves on his hands, black boots, and a wool cap on his head. A pair of thick, wide glasses covered most of his face, and it looked to Newton like the rest of his face was bandaged. And that wasn't all. Newton saw something green and gooey dripping down from one of the kid's sleeves.

"Higglesworth Goodrich Vollington the Eighth, but you can call me Higgy," the boy said. He took a step forward, and his foot made a *pffffft* sound when it touched the floor. It kind of sounded like Higgy had passed gas, but it was actually the squishy sound his feet made whenever he walked.

Cool! Newton thought.

Higgy reached out to Newton, and Newton responded, expecting to shake the rubber-gloved hand. Instead, a tendril of green goo snaked out from under the sleeve and wrapped itself around Newton's palm.

"Um, nice to meet you," Newton replied. "Newton Warp."

"Nice to meet you, too," Higgy said pleasantly. "Come in and check out our humble abode."

Newton stepped into the room and Higgy closed the door behind him. Newton wasn't sure what a "humble abode" was, but if it meant "big mess," then he figured that would make sense. There were clothes, bandages, and rubber gloves strewn all over the floor. There was a desk, but it was covered with books, papers, and empty snack bags. Next to the desk was a plain wooden dresser covered with stickers.

Higgy moved to the dresser, making the same sound

as before with each step—*pffft! pffft! pffft!*—and opened the top drawer.

"I cleaned out a drawer for you," he said.

"For what?" Newton asked.

"For your clothes and things, of course," Higgy replied. Then he looked to the left and right of Newton. "Oh, but it looks like you didn't bring any luggage."

"No, just this," Newton replied. He held up the drawstring bag Mumtaz had given him. "Ms. Mumtaz said she gave me some spirit wear."

Newton opened the bag for the first time and pulled out a yellow T-shirt with the words FRANKEN-SCI HIGH emblazoned on it in lime green. There were lime-green shorts to match, trimmed in bright yellow. He tried to imagine what he would look like wearing them, and a word popped into his mind.

Uncool.

"That's not a bad start," Higgy said. Another green tendril snaked out and plucked the bag out of Newton's hand. Then it stretched until it reached the drawer and dropped the bag inside.

"You know, if you need to borrow some clothes until your luggage gets here, you can borrow some of mine," Higgy offered. He picked up a shirt off the floor, shiny with green goo.

"No, thanks," Newton said quickly.

Then Higgy pointed to the top bunk. "I cleared that off for you too."

"Thanks!" Newton said. Then he quickly scurried up to the top bunk in a flash. He kicked off his shoes, and they fell to the floor with a clatter.

"Whoa, you can really move," Higgy said, impressed.

Newton sat on the mattress and bounced a little. It felt pretty comfortable.

"So, you're new here?" Higgy asked him.

"Yes," Newton replied. "It's my first day."

"Well, I hope you like it here better than I do," Higgy said. "I mean, most kids are thrilled to be here, but they came here by choice. Mum and Dad sent me here after some *rather* unfortunate disciplinary issues I had at home. They thought I'd fit in better at a place like this."

"So why don't you like it?" Newton asked.

"Everyone here thinks they're some kind of genius," Higgy replied. "Yet they're not open-minded enough to befriend someone who's a little different. I'm made of protoplasm, you see."

"You mean that green stuff?" Newton asked.

Higgy nodded. "From head to toe! My whole body is a gelatinous mass of green goo. These garments seem to make it easier for typical-looking people to accept me.

And of course, they also help to hold me together."

Newton nodded. "I can see that."

"The truth is, I'm afraid I don't behave very well when people have a bad attitude about my appearance," Higgy went on.

"You don't?" Newton asked.

"What's the matter?" Higgy challenged. "Are *you* going to have a problem with a roommate made of goo?"

"No, that's not it at all!" Newton said. "It's just . . . I'm not exactly a normal kid either, so I wonder if I'll have the same problem."

Curious, Higgy moved closer and sat on the edge of the bottom bunk. "You look normal enough."

"Yeah, well, I'm not really sure what I'm doing here," Newton replied.

Higgy leaned back on his bed. "You and me both, Newton," he said. "I mean, I know Mum and Dad were upset when I got in trouble sometimes, but I never thought they'd send me away. I really miss them. But I especially miss my little brother, Wellington. He's still with them in England."

Newton clasped his hands behind his head and leaned back. "At least you *have* a family," he admitted. "I woke up in the library a few hours ago and have no idea who I am or where I came from. So I might have a family out there somewhere, and they might be worr—"

Click!

Zzzzzzzzzz!

Newton stopped. *What was that clicking sound? And is that snoring? Did Higgy fall asleep?*

"Higgy?" he asked, and he jumped down from the bunk.

Blop!

Newton's feet landed in a huge pile of green goo. It squished between his toes and looked just like—

"Oh no!" Newton cried. "Higgy! Are you all right?"

When there was no answer, Newton reached down and touched the goo. It didn't feel quite as slimy as when he'd shaken Higgy's tendril, and it smelled kind of sweet.

Zzzzzzzzz . . .

The snoring was coming from the bottom bunk, but Higgy wasn't there. Instead, Newton found a small device—smaller than the school-issued tablet—with a recorded snoring sound coming from it.

Zzzzzzzzz . . .

He suddenly understood that Higgy must be playing a trick on him—pranking him—and that the goo on the floor must be fake goo. That was a relief! But where was the real Higgy?

That's when he noticed that some of the mounds of dirty clothes in front of the bed had been pushed aside. He got down on his knees, peered under the bottom bunk, and saw that a path had been cleared between the piles of stuff.

Newton snaked under the bed. It was dark, and at first he couldn't see much of anything. Then suddenly his eyes adjusted and he could see very clearly that the path led to a small, wide trapdoor!

Newton pressed a button next to the door and it slid to the side with a *click*. Newton realized that must have been the clicking sound he heard earlier.

He wiggled through the opening, landing in a tube that sloped downward until it reached a large tunnel under the dorm building that branched off in different directions.

"Higgy!" he called in a loud whisper. "Where are you?" Nothing.

Then all of a sudden there was a loud, echoing, "Boo!" and something bounced out of one of the tunnel's branches and rolled toward Newton.

He jumped up, terrified, and instinctively stretched out his arms and legs. They stuck to the ceiling! From his perch up there, he looked down and saw that what scared him was actually a gelatinous ball of goo.

Then two eyeballs popped out of it.

"Sorry I scared you, Newton," the goo ball gurgled. "But that's one cool trick you can do."

Newton hopped to the ground. "Higgy?"

"Yup. It's me," Higgy replied. "I ditched my clothes. Without them, I can basically shift into any form I want to. Comes in handy."

"Wow, that's pretty cool," Newton remarked.

"Thanks," Higgy replied. "And that means you passed the roommate test!"

"I did?" Newton asked.

"Yup," Higgy replied. "You didn't run screaming, and you knew it was me. My last roommate dropped out of school and never looked back."

I can understand that, Newton thought. He looked around. "So what is this place?"

"I've studied these underground tunnels and they lead to every section of the school," Higgy explained. "I built the trapdoor so I could sneak into the cafeteria for midnight snacks without getting caught. I seem to have a much greater caloric requirement than other kids do. Guess it's a goo thing."

Newton nodded. "Which one leads to the cafeteria?"

Higgy turned on a flashlight he was holding and pointed it at one of the tunnels. "That one leads to the cafeteria and the locker hives. The one over there leads to the library, but I've never felt the urge for a midnight study session."

Higgy started to bounce down the cafeteria tunnel. "Follow me! I know it's not midnight yet, but all this activity has made me crave calories."

Newton followed as Higgy bounced and slithered down the tunnel. Newton looked around as they went.

The floor beneath them felt hard and smooth. Above, the ceiling looked like wood. Pipes snaked along the tunnel walls, some of them dripping water. Lacy spider-webs hung in the corners.

The tunnel came to a turn, and Higgy stopped and looked up. A large round pipe hung down from the ceiling.

"This leads to the cafeteria's kitchen," Higgy said. "I can just slither right up, and if you can scurry up it like you did with the bunk bed, I think you'll make it."

"Sure," Newton said, and he realized he was excited. Sharing this secret with Higgy . . . sharing secrets was something that friends did. He'd found another friend.

Then they heard a loud creaking noise.

"Hold up!" Higgy whispered, and he flattened himself against the wall. Newton did the same thing.

Then one of Higgy's eyeballs extended on a tendril of goo and peeked around the corner.

"It's Stubbins Crouch!" Higgy whispered. "What's he doing down here?"

"Who's that?" Newton whispered back.

"The school custodian," Higgy replied. "He cleans up the place. But this is the first time I've seen him down here."

Higgy was silent for a moment. "He went toward the Teacher's Lounge," he said. "But it's not safe. I

wish we could get something to eat, but I'm afraid we should go back."

"Sure," Newton said.

They made their way back toward the dorm room and up through the trapdoor. Higgy bounced onto his bed.

"I hope you don't mind if I sleep in my gooey state," Higgy said.

"That's fine with me," Newton said, and climbed back onto the top of the bunk again. Then he leaned back on the pillow.

"Hey, Higgy?"

"What?"

"Your last roommate left the school and never came back?" Newton asked.

"That's right," Higgy replied. "He was totally spine-less. And I can say that because I don't have a spine and I'm a lot tougher than he was!"

Newton thought about that for a minute. Higgy must have really scared his last roommate. But he seemed like a good guy at heart.

"Good night, Higgy."

"Good night, Newton."

Then Newton closed his eyes.

CHAPTER 6

It's Alive!

"Rise and shine, Newton!"

As Newton heard Higgy's cheerful voice and opened his eyes, Shelly's words from the day before popped into his head.

Maybe tomorrow you'll wake up and remember everything.

"I'm Newton Warp," he said out loud, testing it. He knew he was at Franken-Sci High. He knew he was in a dorm room with his roommate, Higgy, who was made of green goo. He remembered everything that happened after he woke up in the library yesterday—but nothing at all that happened before. And he felt a new feeling: disappointment.

He didn't have time to dwell on it, though, because Higgy was staring at him, dressed in his bandages and clothes again.

"I already know your name, Newton," Higgy said.

"Just wanted to let you know that it's six forty-five. And yesterday I overheard you talking to Shelly Ravenholt outside the door. She'll be here in fifteen minutes."

Newton jumped down from the top bunk. "Thanks," he said, and then started hopping from side to side on alternating feet and then dancing toward the door to their room. "Uh . . ."

"Bathroom is down the hall on the left," Higgy said.

Newton was back and dressed in his spirit wear when Shelly knocked on the door at 7:00 a.m. on the dot.

"Happy day two!" she said when he answered the door. "Did any memories come back to you?"

Newton shook his head. "None," he said.

Shelly gave him a sympathetic smile. "That's okay. Today we can make lots of new ones."

Newton smiled. He liked the sound of that.

Then she looked him up and down. "And maybe we'll find you some new clothes, too," she said. "Not that what you're wearing isn't . . . spirited. Come on, we'll grab a quick smoothie first."

He grabbed his bag and tablet, and they made their way to the main school building and up a transport tube to the cafeteria. Newton smoothed his hair without thinking this time.

Shelly led him through a crowd of students to a big

metal machine on one side of the cafeteria. She grabbed a large paper cup, placed it under a nozzle, and pressed a button.

"I'm getting a Morning Maximizer for each of us," she said. "Each smoothie is calculated to have enough protein, minerals, and amino acids to get us through to lunchtime."

She put a straw in the cup and handed the smoothie to Newton. Then she made herself one.

"Let's take the stairs," she said, leading Newton to a spiral staircase. "The last time I tried to take a smoothie in a transport tube, the lid flew off and my smoothie went everywhere. Stubbins Crouch, the school custodian, was furious at me."

They slurped their smoothies as they took the steps down to the first floor. Shelly led him to a group of bins outside Mumtaz's office.

She tossed her cup into a bin marked COMPOST. Newton did the same. Then Shelly pointed to another bin marked LOST AND FOUND.

"Some of the stuff has been in here for years," Shelly said, digging into the pile. "I bet we can find you a whole wardrobe."

A pile started to form at Newton's feet as Shelly tossed things to him. Gray-and-black spider-print shorts with a belt that doubled as a butterfly net. Neon-green galoshes. Black jeans that self-adjusted to fit anyone perfectly at the touch of a button. A hazmat suit. A few T-shirts, including one with built-in air-conditioning. A jacket.

"I don't see any socks, but I can knit you some," Shelly said. She yanked on the scarf she was wearing. "It's a hobby."

"Thanks," Newton said, picking up the clothes.

"No time to go back to your dorm," Shelly said. "I'm

taking you to a Monster Club meeting before our first class. Let's dump these in your locker for now."

At the locker hive, Newton was pleased that he remembered the opening procedure: fingerprint, eyeballs, and then . . .

"Whoa!" he said, licking the pad. "It tastes like . . . fire, and something sour, and other stuff."

"I haven't opened my locker yet, but I hear it's kimchi," Shelly explained. Newton looked confused. "It's a spicy, fermented cabbage used in Korean food."

"I like it," Newton said as he stuffed the clothes in his locker and shut the door. Then he followed Shelly as they rushed to the club meeting.

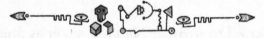

They walked into a cozy laboratory filled with illustrated posters of plant and animal species, beakers and petri dishes balanced precariously on towering piles of paper, and students checking on a variety of experiments in progress. Professor Gertrude Leviathan, a woman with a wild mass of pink curls framing her face and a leopard-print lab coat, was bustling around from table to table, greeting everyone. When she saw Shelly, she rushed over and gave her a big hug.

"Hello, my dear!" she said. "I see you've brought a

friend! How marvelous!"

"Yes, this is Newton," Shelly replied. "He's a new student. You didn't get a message about him from Mumtaz?"

Leviathan pointed to the messy pile on her desk. "I haven't checked my messages today. Can't find my tablet," she said. "But I'm ecstatic to have you here, Newton. We're a Franken-Science Club. Do you know what that is?" she asked, but didn't wait for him to answer. "It's all about bringing things to life and making monsters, and it's wonderful! We've been working on animating everyday things that aren't usually alive. You know, making toothbrushes sing, desk lamps dance, and those sorts of things. You'll pick it up in no time!"

Shelly and Newton found seats as the club meeting began. "How are everyone's formulas coming along?" Leviathan asked.

The students all answered, mostly in a positive way, and one girl boomed, "Great!" Newton turned at the sound of her loud voice. He saw a girl whose hair was tied in a braided bun on top of her head.

"That's Tootie Van der Flootin," Shelly told Newton. "She's a big fan of *mutant* monster making. Not my style, really, but she's basically okay."

"Don't forget to have fun, everyone," Professor

Leviathan announced, "and raise your hand if you need help."

The kids got busy working. Shelly's formula was already completed, and applied to a pair of pet food and water bowls that were growing in the incubator.

"It's a machine that provides a controlled environment to help things grow," she told Newton. She let him take a peek, and the bowls were already starting to move on their own.

"Hi!" Newton said to the food bowl, and it let out a little *arf*!

Tootie walked up to Shelly and nodded at Newton. "'Sup, new kid?"

"'Sup," Newton replied.

"Wait till you guys see the totally fierce monster I'm working on for the Mad Science Fair!" Tootie said. "It's going to be terrifyingly awesome."

Shelly shivered. "You know I don't do scary, Tootie," Shelly said.

"You're missing out." Tootie said. "It's a blast. Speaking of which, I need to get going on my experiment."

Shelly brightened. "Hey, can we watch you work on it? Mine's in the incubator."

Tootie shrugged. "Sure."

Newton and Shelly watched as Tootie started mixing

ingredients, heating them on a hot plate, using a centri-fuge to separate liquid, and compiling a small mountain of test tubes and pipettes. Finally, a miniature firework burst out of a vial of green liquid, and Tootie said it was ready.

"What's it for?" Newton asked.

Tootie smiled. "It's a surprise. But don't worry: You'll find out later today. I have a special test planned."

The bell rang, and Shelly looked at Newton. "Ready for your first class?"

Newton nodded. "I think so. It's just . . . I guess I'm worried that I won't know anything. I don't even know if I've ever been in a class!"

They walked down the hall and stopped in front of a wooden door. "I'm sure Mumtaz has told the teachers about your amnesia," Shelly said. "Don't stress about it."

She opened the door, and the room was filled with kids getting settled at their desks. They all looked up when Shelly and Newton walked in.

"You must be Newton. Come over here, young man."

Newton turned to see a man sitting behind a desk. Wisps of white hair sprouted from his head like weeds. His wire spectacles were enormous on his thin, wrinkled face and made his eyes look huge. He was dressed neatly, but everything he wore clashed. He was

wearing yellow-and-orange tartan pants, a blue-and-green checked shirt, purple plaid suspenders, and a red gingham bowtie.

"This is Newton Warp, Professor Wagg," Shelly said. "He needs a textbook."

"Warp, eh?" Professor Wagg repeated in a creaky voice. "Where are you from, young man?"

"Um . . . the library," Newton answered, and some of the students tittered.

Professor Wagg sighed. "Another disrespectful young scamp. Take a seat, please." He handed a book to Newton: *A Comprehensive History of Mad Scientists from the Pyramids to the Present.*

"Most of our textbooks are files on our tablets," Shelly explained while they walked to their seats. "But Professor Wagg is old school."

Newton slid into his seat—and then heard a loud voice next to him.

"Good morning, Newton-who-is-*not*-a-spy." It was Mimi. "I think it's interesting that even though you *say* you're not a spy, you chose to sit right next to me where you can see everything I do."

"Um, I'm actually sitting next to Shelly," Newton said, pointing to Shelly next to him.

"Likely story," Mimi said.

There was a *beep* sound. After two more beeps, a holographic image of Headmistress Mumtaz's head appeared in the front of the room.

"Good morning, students," she said. "I want to remind everyone that the annual Mad Science Fair is only two weeks away. By now you should have completed your hypotheses and begun the testing process. A reminder: Any projects involving carnivorous creatures must be pre-approved by the main office. Stay tuned for tomorrow, when we will announce this year's big prize. Happy experimenting and good luck!"

Mumtaz's holographic head flickered, then disappeared, and all the students began to chatter excitedly.

"Don't get too excited about the prize, everyone, because it's going to be *mine*," Mimi announced loudly. Then she turned to Newton. "And don't bother asking me what my project is, because it's top secret." She turned toward Newton. "What's *your* project? Some kind of spy technology?"

"I . . . I don't know," Newton admitted. He turned to Shelly. "Am I supposed to come up with a project?"

"I'm not sure," she said, "but usually everyone participates. Don't worry, you can team up with me and Theremin. We're still trying to come up with an idea, but I think we're close."

Professor Wagg cleared his throat. "Let's turn to chapter fourteen, class. 'Mad Scientists Who Were Eaten By Their Experiments.'"

For the rest of the class, the professor lectured. His voice was dry and boring, but Newton was riveted by the stories of carnivorous flowers and ravenous porch swings. He was relieved that he was able to follow along even though it was his first class ever, as far as he knew.

Then the bell rang.

"Next class," Shelly announced. "Bending Electricity Safely."

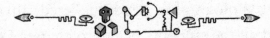

Shelly led Newton to the classroom. In the front, there was a very small desk with a chair shaped like a fuzzy bear. Sitting in the chair was a young girl in a crisp white lab coat. She wore her red hair in braids that hung down her back and was busily typing on a computer.

"Professor Juvinall?" Shelly asked.

The girl's head snapped up.

"This must be Newton Warp," she said flatly. "Just got the notice. Shelly, I'm assuming you'll stay with him today?"

Shelly nodded. "If that's okay."

Newton kept staring at the professor. "You're little!"

he blurted out without thinking.

Professor Juvinall glared at him. "Of course I am. I'm six years old. And smarter than you'll ever be. So that's the last I want to hear about that. Understand?"

Newton nodded and followed Shelly to a lab table.

"Sorry," Shelly whispered to him. "I should have warned you."

As they took their seats on metal stools, Newton saw something that made his mouth drop open. It was a brain in a jar, and it was coming toward them. It was different than the brains Newton had seen in the library. For starters, it was perched on a table with a tall, metal leg and wheels on the bottom. It also seemed to be alive, accompanied by a skinny boy with greasy black hair that swooped down over his forehead.

"Finally you meet—well, the *brain* is Odifin," Shelly whispered, as the jar came closer, "and the one *without* a brain is Rotwang."

"Stop right there, Shelly," Odifin said. His voice came through a speaker at the base of his jar.

"Yeah, stop right there," Rotwang echoed.

"Odifin. Rotwang. What do you two want?" Shelly asked.

"You tried to get me in trouble with Headmistress

Mumtaz," Odifin responded. "Claiming that I would waste some of my precious experimental amnesia formula on a new student."

"That's me, hi," Newton said, giving a small wave.

"I informed her that I did no such thing," Odifin snapped. "My amnesia formula is not even ready for testing yet. Only an irresponsible scientist would test a formula prematurely."

"Yeah, irrebonkable," parroted Rotwang.

"Sorry, Odifin," Shelly said. "It was just a guess. I was trying to help Newton here, and well, since you had an amnesia formula and he has amnesia, it seemed possible."

"So the newbie has amnesia, does he?" Odifin asked. He rolled right up to Newton's face, and the liquid inside the brain jar began to bubble. "Interesting. Very interesting."

"Yeah, very interesting," Rotwang repeated.

"Are we done here?" Shelly asked.

"Maybe we are done," Odifin said. "And maybe we are not."

Then he rolled over to another lab table, followed by Rotwang.

"Well, there goes that theory," Shelly said to Newton. "Presuming that Odifin is telling the truth, of course."

"Who's that kid with him?" Newton asked.

"Rotwang?" Shelly asked. "He's been held back, like, six times. I don't even think he's a teenager anymore. He comes from a long line of mad scientist assistants."

"What do assistants do?" Newton wondered.

Shelly thought for a moment. "I guess you could say they do whatever mad scientists tell them to do."

Newton raised his eyebrows. "Do you have an assistant?" he asked.

Shelly shook her head. Before Newton could reply, Professor Juvinall's voice rang out.

"Goggles and rubber gloves on, everyone!" the professor yelled. "This class isn't called Bending Electricity Safely for nothing! Even so, do *not* try this at home."

Professor Juvinall barked out instructions for some kind of experiment, but Newton was completely confused. Shelly did most of the work at their table, connecting wires and making lights flash on and off.

Even so, Professor Juvinall kept calling on Newton.

"Warp! Is that a positive or negative charge?"

"Warp! How can we make sure a wire is properly grounded?"

"Warp! Can you predict if the blue light or the red light will go on first?"

Newton had no idea how to answer any of the questions, and was relieved when Shelly answered for him.

After the third question, he heard Odifin's crackling voice snort from across the room. "I guess we do not have to worry about competition from this guy," he said loudly, and a lot of students laughed.

When the bell rang again, Newton left the room as fast as he could.

"That was really hard," he told Shelly as they emerged into the hall.

"That might be a tough class to begin with, especially since things started off on the wrong foot with Juvinall," Shelly agreed. "I was thinking you might want to take Neo-Evolutionary Biology."

"Why? Is that easier?" Newton asked.

"I just think it might come more . . . naturally to you," Shelly answered mysteriously. "But the good news is, we have a break in your schedule before lunchtime, and I want to show you something."

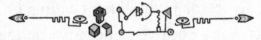

Shelly took Newton to the basement of the building.

"This is my little secret," she said. "Mumtaz is letting me keep rescue animals down here."

She opened a door, and Newton's eyes grew wide. The room was full of all kinds of tropical animals.

"This is Wingold," she said, showing him a parrot

with a robotic wing to assist a wing that had been badly injured. "He's almost ready to be released into the wild."

"Hello! Hello!" said Wingold.

"Hi!" replied Newton.

"Theremin helped me refine the robotic wing so it's actually better than the original," Shelly added.

There was also a sea turtle with a titanium shell, a frog with springs to replace its missing hind legs, and more.

"This is so cool," Newton said.

"It's just the beginning," Shelly said, filling up the animals' automatic food dispensers. "But it's almost time for

lunch. If we leave now, we'll have time to get on the hot lunch line before they're out of fungus fries!"

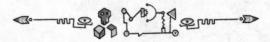

They rode in the tube up to the cafeteria, got in line, and filled their plates with food.

"We should get broccoli and fungus fries for both of us," Shelly informed Newton. "And Chicken Surprise for you. I don't eat meat, but everyone says the Chicken Surprise is pretty good."

She navigated through the crowded lunchroom toward a table where Theremin was sitting. As soon as he saw Newton, Theremin's face dropped.

"Oh, is *he* sitting with us?" Theremin grumbled.

"Of course he is," Shelly said. "Who else is he going to sit with?"

Theremin grunted and stared down at his empty plate.

"It's nice to see you again, Theremin," Newton said, sliding into his seat. Then he started digging in to his food.

"Mmm, these fungus fries are good," he remarked.

"Told you," Shelly said. Then she turned to Theremin. "So, I told Newton he could work on our science fair project with us."

"Wait, what?" Theremin asked. "No way!"

Shelly glared at him. "Let's talk about this later, okay?"

Newton looked away, feeling embarrassed.

Why doesn't Theremin like me? he wondered.

His gaze wandered to the table next to them, where he noticed Tootie and some of the other kids from the Monster Club. They were whispering and giggling. Then Newton saw that Tootie was holding an electrical gauge with wires attached to their plates, and little sparks were flying.

"What are they doing?" Newton asked.

Before Shelly could answer, Tootie stood up and yelled, "Food fight!"

She tossed a stalk of broccoli through the air. It landed on another table and started running around— on tiny green legs!

A glob of Chicken Surprise landed in front of Newton. Two eyes opened up on the glob of casserole, and a little mouth formed a circle of surprise.

"Now wasn't *that* surprising!" the Chicken Surprise said.

Newton stared in amazement. Over at the next table, a slab of meatloaf was arguing with a bottle of ketchup.

"I don't need you!" the meatloaf was saying. "Sometimes I just gotta be me!"

Shelly was laughing. "This happens every time someone learns how to bring their lunch to life," she said. "It's so—duck!"

Another broccoli stalk landed in front of Newton.

"Why does nobody like me?" the broccoli wailed. "I'm loaded with nutrition and an excellent source of vitamin C!"

"It never lasts long, but it's kind of contagious," Shelly explained, looking down at Newton's fungus fries. They had started to jump up and down. "Pretty soon it will just be regular food again."

Theremin tapped Shelly on the shoulder. "Shelly, about him . . ." Theremin nodded toward Newton. "I don't want to talk about it later."

Shelly ignored him. Instead, she held out her plate of fries to Newton.

"Want some of mine? I got extra," she said.

"Sure," Newton replied. He reached out to grab the plate from Shelly. . . .

Theremin's eyes flashed green. He intercepted the plate, picked up the fungus fries, and hurled them at Newton's face.

"You want fries? Have some fries!"

At that, those fries came to life too and began to pummel Newton's face. It tickled, and he started laughing.

"I get it. The food *fights*!" Newton said. Then he picked up a ketchup bottle from the table, aimed it at Theremin, and squeezed until ketchup squirted out.

"Weeeeeeee," the ketchup squealed with delight.

But when it landed on Theremin, there was a sizzling sound, and steam streamed out of the robot's neck.

"He's trying to deactivate me!" Theremin screamed.

"He didn't know!" Shelly cried. She jumped up and started wiping off the ketchup with napkins.

"What did I do?" Newton asked.

"The acid in the ketchup can cause Theremin's wires to short out," Shelly explained. "But you had no way of knowing that. It's okay."

"It is NOT okay," Theremin fumed. He floated backward, knocking the chair to the ground. "And I do not understand why you, Shelly Ravenholt, my best friend, would want to hang out with a kid who is trying to—to—KILL me!"

"Theremin, it was an accident," Shelly said pleadingly. "And you *did* throw a plate of fries at his face."

Theremin stormed out of the lunchroom, too angry to listen.

Newton frowned. *Maybe there's a reason I forgot who I am,* he thought. *Maybe it's because I could never do anything right!*

CHAPTER 7

Use Your Noodle Noggin!

Shelly's voice interrupted Newton's thoughts.

"You don't have a scheduled class next period," she said. "So why don't you stick with me? It's a pretty cool class. Theremin and I both really like it."

"I don't know," Newton said. "I don't think Theremin wants to see me right now."

"Theremin will cool down," Shelly promised. "He always does. And anyway, the class is about genetics—the study of how biological characteristics are passed on from one generation to the next. Who knows? Maybe we'll learn something that can help us figure out where you're from."

"Sure, let's go," he said.

He followed her to another classroom set up like a lab. The teacher, Thaddeus Wells, was waiting by the front door when Shelly and Newton walked in.

"Ah, Newton Warp. Nice to see you in this dimension.

Wasn't sure which one you'd be walking into," he said.

Newton noticed something strange about the teacher. Half of Wells's body looked like a normal body, with a round face, a tiny mustache, and thin brown hair. But the other half looked . . . well, fuzzy. It kind of flickered in and out, like it wasn't solid.

"Newton isn't scheduled for this class, Professor Wells, but I'm showing him around today, so I brought him with me," Shelly explained.

"Excellent! Please have him sit next to you," he said. Newton noticed then that the teacher was talking out of the solid side of his mouth. In the very next instant, he spoke from the fuzzy side of his mouth.

"Abigail Belowvich, get off the ceiling!"

Newton looked up at the ceiling. There was nothing there. He threw Shelly a puzzled look as they sat down.

"Oh right," she said. "Professor Wells was caught in a nasty interdimensional portal accident. So, half of him is in this dimension, and the other half is in a parallel dimension—like, a place that's exactly like this one, only right next to us, and we can't see it."

Newton nodded.

"The good news is that he can teach two classes at the same time," Shelly explained. "One in this dimension, and one in the other."

At that moment Theremin floated into the room. His eyes turned green again when he spotted Shelly and Newton.

"That's—MY—seat," Theremin said.

Shelly patted the stool on her other side. "You can sit here."

Theremin grunted and floated over to the stool. Then Professor Wells began to talk out of both sides of his mouth.

"Good morning, classes," he said. "I'd like to begin with a pop quiz on chapter two of your *Genetic Friendgineering* books."

Some of the students groaned. Shelly leaned over to Newton. "Genetic Friendgineering is when you manipulate the genes of your friends, so that they're more compatible with your own personality traits," she said. "Take out your tablet and click on the professor's name. You'll find the book there."

Professor Wells spoke out of the solid side of his mouth. "Mr. Warp, since you are new, you don't have to take the quiz. Please start reading chapter one of the textbook so you can catch up to us."

"Sure, sir," Newton replied.

Newton took out his tablet and followed Shelly's instructions. The other students turned on their tablets.

The quiz popped up on their screens, and everyone got to work.

After fifteen minutes, everyone's tablets beeped. Their screens went blank. Professor Wells started typing on his laptop with his left hand. His right hand disappeared into the other dimension.

"Class, begin reading chapter three while I grade these," he said.

Newton was still reading chapter one, but he was enjoying it. Things were starting to click in his mind. He wasn't sure if he was remembering things he'd learned before or was just learning them now.

"Classes, I have your scores," Professor Wells said out of both mouths. Numbers started popping up on the tablets of the students who'd taken the quiz.

Newton glanced over at Shelly. Her screen flashed **95**. Theremin's screen flashed **100**.

"Uh-oh," Shelly muttered under her breath. "He got a perfect score."

"Wow, great job, Theremin!" Newton said, and instinctively he raised his hand to give the robot a high-five.

"Whatever," Theremin grumbled, and Newton figured that Theremin was still mad at him.

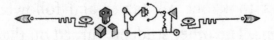

When the bell rang, Newton waited for Theremin to float out of the room. Then he turned to Shelly.

"Theremin didn't look happy about his good grade," Newton said. "Is he still mad at me?"

"It's not that," Shelly replied. "It's his programming."

She explained how Theremin's dad had made sure that Theremin could never be smarter than him.

"So every time Theremin does really well, it means he's going to do really badly at the next thing he tries," Shelly explained. "But you'll see for yourself in our next class."

The next class was Dark Matter Matters, taught by Professor Anatoly Phlegm. The bottom of his black lab coat touched the floor, he wore black gloves up to his elbows and a black patch over his right eye, and his head was completely bald and shiny under the fluorescent lights.

Professor Phlegm nodded curtly to Newton after Shelly introduced him, and Newton found an empty desk next to Shelly again.

"You will have fifteen minutes to look over yesterday's notes," Professor Phlegm announced. "And then we will quiz you."

Shelly raised her hand. "Professor Phlegm, it's Newton's first day. Can he be excused from the quiz?"

"No, he may not," Professor Phlegm replied. "He's a

member of our class, just like everyone else."

Then he looked directly at Newton. "He just needs to use his . . . ahem . . . noodle noggin."

Noodle noggin. The words jolted Newton. But why did they sound so familiar?

"I'll send you the notes," Shelly said. She tapped her tablet and notes popped up on Newton's screen.

"Thanks," Newton said.

He started to read, but he heard Theremin whispering to Shelly.

"Shelly, you know I'm going to fail this," he hissed.

"Well, let's try a few basic questions to see how you do," Shelly said hopefully. "What's ten plus five?"

"Albuquerque?" Theremin guessed.

Shelly sighed. "Yeah, looks like you're going to fail. But don't let it get to you. There's always next time!"

Theremin grunted.

Newton began to read the notes that Shelly had given him. He was surprised at himself. He understood everything perfectly!

When it came time for the quiz, Newton's fingers were a blur as he confidently tapped his answers into the tablet.

Because it was a multiple-choice test, Professor Phlegm graded it with the touch of a button on his laptop. Grades popped up on everyone's screens.

Theremin: **0**

Shelly: **89**

Newton: **100**

"Excellent work, Mr. Warp," Professor Phlegm said. "You seem to have absorbed the material very quickly." He sounded very pleased by this.

"Thanks," Newton said. "But I don't understand. How did I—"

Shelly interrupted him. "You must be a quick learner!" she said. "Way to go, Newton!"

There was a crash as Theremin threw his tablet across the room and floated out the door, his eyes flashing green with jealousy.

"We're not amused, Mr. Rozika!" Professor Phlegm yelled after him.

Shelly explained that it was the last class of the day, so they had some time to work on homework or relax before dinner. She hoped Theremin would cool off.

"You know, maybe I should give Theremin some space," Newton said. "I'll find someone else to eat dinner with tonight."

Shelly frowned. "Who?"

"I could eat with Higgy," Newton suggested.

Shelly raised an eyebrow. "Oh boy. Are you sure?"

Newton shrugged. "Yeah. Why not?"

Newton found out the answer later, after he asked Higgy if they could eat dinner together.

Higgy was thrilled. They went to the cafeteria and filled their plates with hydrogenated spaghetti and macrobiotic meatballs. Higgy piled his plate three times higher than anyone else in the cafeteria. When they sat down, he started shoveling the spaghetti under his face bandages with lightning speed.

Pffft! Pffft! Pffft! When Higgy put the food into his mouth, it made the same sound he made when he walked in his shoes.

Then Newton saw some of the spaghetti strands poking out through the bandages.

"Takes a while to absorb," Higgy said, pushing it back in. "Got to keep it from escaping."

"Um, yeah," said Newton, who was fascinated and disgusted at the same time.

Then Higgy let out an enormous burp, and a green bubble floated out of his mouth.

That's about when Newton noticed that not only was nobody sitting at the table with them, but nobody was sitting at any of the tables near them.

"*Buuuuuuuurp!*" Higgy burped again and stood up. "I just made room for seconds!" he cried.

Newton looked down at his own plate. He had only taken a few bites in the time Higgy had taken to finish a mountain of food.

Then something hopped onto the table right in front of him. It looked like a spider, but it was made of metal!

The mechanical spider scurried along Newton's sleeve. Then the top of the spider's back opened up, and a holographic text message appeared.

Want to sneak into Mumtaz's office tonight? We can check your profile and find out what she's hiding from you! Meet you at 9 at your dorm. SR

The message disappeared as soon as he had read it, and the spider clattered away. Newton watched as it scurried over to Shelly. She caught his eye, smiled, and winked. Newton smiled back.

Maybe tonight I'll finally get some answers about who I really am! he thought hopefully.

CHAPTER 8

The Mumtaz Mission

Later that night, Newton answered the door and saw Shelly there, just as she promised. She had swapped her polka-dot leggings for black ones, and was wearing a black snakelike knit scarf instead of her usual one. But she still wore the furry poncho.

"That's quite a nice look," Higgy said. "But I'm afraid I didn't get the message to wear black."

Shelly walked in and greeted Higgy with mild surprise.

"Don't be shocked, Shelly, our good friend Newton has told me all about your plan," Higgy said. "And I have generously agreed to help you."

Shelly glanced over at Newton. He nodded.

"Higgy knows all about the tunnels underneath the school," Newton told her. "We can sneak into Mumtaz's office without anyone seeing us."

"Underground tunnels? I had no idea," Shelly said.

She looked down at her outfit. "I guess I dressed like a ninja for nothing."

"A rather furry ninja," Higgy remarked.

"Come on!" Newton said eagerly. "Let's go."

"I shall be your guide," Higgy said. "And I hope you don't freak, Shelly, but I work best if I am unfettered."

"Unfettered?" Shelly asked. Higgy slipped out of his coat, boots, bandages, hat, and welder's goggles, revealing his smiley-face boxer shorts and his green, globby self. "Oh."

"To the tunnels!" Higgy cried, and he slithered under the bunk bed.

"Follow me," Newton said, and he crawled after Higgy.

Shelly obeyed and slid under the bed, then dropped down through the trapdoor after Newton.

"It's so dark down here," Shelly said. "I think I have a flashlight here somewhere."

"Really? I can see fine," Newton said.

"You can?" Shelly asked. She produced a flashlight from under her poncho and used it to illuminate the tunnels ahead of them. Higgy was already slithering down one of them, lighting his way with a flashlight of his own.

"This way," Newton whispered.

Shelly looked around as they walked. "Wow. Does

anyone else know these exist?"

"Higgy thinks the teaching staff knows, but the only person he's seen here is the custodian," Newton replied. "It was just last night—but luckily Crouch didn't see us."

Shelly picked up her pace. "We'd better hurry, then."

They caught up to Higgy, who had stopped and pointed up to the ceiling with a green goo tentacle.

"That's the floor grate to Mumtaz's office," he said.

"Great!" Newton said. He jumped up and stuck to the ceiling with his fingertips, not noticing the surprised look on Shelly's face. He pushed open the grate. Then he swung up into the room.

"All clear," he whispered, reaching down to grab Shelly.

"I'll be your lookout down here!" Higgy called up in a loud whisper. One of his eyeballs snaked out to the right on a tentacle-like stalk, and the other one snaked out to the left, so he could see in two directions. "Got you covered!"

Newton helped Shelly to her feet and walked over to Mumtaz's desk.

"She called up the database by swiping the air," he remembered. He tried doing it, but nothing appeared.

"I think it has to be swiped in a precise location," Shelly said. She sat down in the headmistress's chair.

Newton stood next to her. "Mumtaz is about six inches taller than I am. And she reached straight out at about a forty-two degree angle so, if I just reach up six inches . . ."

Before she could try, the sound of footsteps could be heard right outside the door.

"Someone's coming!" Shelly whispered, and she quickly ducked into a nearby closet. "Newton, hide!"

Panicked, he flattened himself against the bookcase behind him, without stopping to think about how it made no sense to hide in plain sight.

The lights flickered on. Headmistress Mumtaz walked in, going right for the desk—and right toward Newton. His mind raced as he tried to think of some excuse he could give her for being in her office.

To his surprise, though, she seemed to look right through him! She slid into her chair and swiped the air, and the database popped up. She scrolled through it quickly (it was nothing interesting; Newton could see it was just an invoice for a dozen Tesla coils). Satisfied, she swiped again, got up, turned off the light, and left the office, locking the door behind her.

Shelly had watched through the gap between the closet doors, and now she slowly came out and stared at Newton.

"That was weird," Newton said. "I could swear she looked right at me, but she didn't even see me."

"Yeah," Shelly said slowly. "Weird is a good word for it."

Newton shrugged. "She must have been tired or something. Or maybe she needs new glasses?"

"Sure, I bet that's it," Shelly replied coolly. "Anyway, the good news is that I saw where she swiped!"

Shelly sat back in the chair and swiped the air. The holographic screen instantly appeared. Newton watched Shelly scroll to the database, but when she tried to access it, a box popped up.

CLASSIFIED. BIOIDENTIFICATION REQUIRED.

Shelly frowned. "It's like the lockers. Probably needs her fingerprint, eyeball scan—something."

"No!" Newton cried. "Come on, there has to be another way!"

He jabbed at the screen with his finger. A new box popped up.

BIOIDENTIFICATION FAILED.

"No fair!" Newton yelled in frustration. He tapped the screen again . . . and again . . .

THIRD ATTEMPT FAILED. PROTOCOLS ACTIVATED.

Suddenly, the ceiling lit up with electrical circuitry. Lines of blue electricity snaked down the walls, covering the window and the door.

"The grate!" Shelly cried, and she grabbed Newton's

hand. While the electricity blocked the windows and the door, it didn't touch the floor. They swiftly descended down the grate and Newton pulled it back into place.

"Let me guess," Higgy said when they were back in the tunnel. "It didn't go well."

"Not exactly," Newton said. "Come on!"

They raced through the tunnels and emerged back in Newton and Higgy's room.

"I'm sorry," Shelly said, smoothing out her furry poncho. "I should have figured she would have the database protected somehow. Everything here is."

"It's okay," Newton replied, but it really wasn't. He felt totally defeated.

"I'll see you in the morning, Newton," Shelly said. "Good night, Higgy."

"Nighty-night!" Higgy said. He'd put his glasses back on and shaped his gooey form inside a bathrobe.

As Shelly left, Newton turned to Higgy. "I think I need a shower," he said. "I can't remember the last time I had one. Literally."

"Sure thing, roomie," Higgy said.

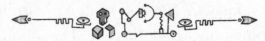

Newton felt better after the shower. The soap from the dispenser smelled minty, and a robot arm handed him

a clean towel when he was done. He slipped into some pajamas (from the Lost and Found pile) and went back to his room.

"Higgy, I—ah!" he screamed when he opened the door.

Green goo dropped on his head from above the door and slid down his hair and onto his face. Then some of it touched his tongue, and Newton realized it tasted sweet.

"Fake goo again?" Newton asked. "What is it?"

"Lime-green jelly," Higgy replied, laughing. "I get it on my midnight runs to the cafeteria. They have vats of it over there."

Newton sighed. "Guess I'll shower again!"

A few minutes later he came back. This time, he carefully opened the door. He scanned the floor for traps. Then he quickly took one jump into the room and scurried up to his bed. He checked the sheets for goo first, before scooting under them.

"No jelly this time?" he asked.

"I thought I'd go easy on you," Higgy said. "It's only your second day, after all."

"Thanks, Higgy," Newton said. As he rolled over in the bed, something caught his eye: The school brochure was sticking out of his bag.

Newton scurried down and grabbed it, then brought

it back up to the top bunk.

"Higgy, the brochure portal—Shelly says it's how you get in the school. Do you also use it to get out?" Newton asked.

"Yes, but you need a portal pass to do it," Higgy replied. "The school doesn't want kids just popping in and out at random. And normally the pass has limits— it usually just sends you back home for a visit. And you need your parents to sign a permission slip. Why, do you want to go somewhere?"

Newton thought about it. "I'm not sure *where* I would go. Right now, this is the only home I know about. Besides, I still can't make the portal work."

Newton opened the brochure, then tried to fold it the way Shelly had showed him, pressing hard on the paper as he got more and more frustrated. Like before, his fingers kept sticking to the paper. He peeled them off and stuffed the brochure back in his bag, frustrated.

"Well, don't feel bad," Higgy said. "My parents don't even want me home until the holidays."

"That stinks," Newton said, then quickly added, "But I'm sure they're just busy and will be really happy to see you over the break, you know? What if I have parents, or brothers and sisters out there who want me to visit? And I can't remember who they are, or where they live,

or even what they look like?"

Higgy bounced out of his bunk. "Maybe your dad looks like you, just taller," he said. He morphed his gooey form into a tall guy with wavy hair like Newton's.

Newton smiled. "Yeah."

"Or maybe he's the exact opposite," Higgy said, reshaping himself into a short man with a baseball cap.

"Hmm," said Newton. "Who knows?"

"And how about your mom?" Higgy asked. He transformed again, into a woman with shoulder-length hair.

"She looks nice," Newton said.

Higgy reshaped back into his own squat, gooey form.

"I can take the form of all the professors, too," he said. "Wanna see?"

Newton yawned. "Maybe tomorrow," he said. "I'm beat."

"No problem, roomie," Higgy said.

A green goo tendril snaked out and shut off the light switch. The room went dark.

"Higgy?" Newton asked.

"What?"

"Thanks," Newton said. "That was nice of you."

Then he closed his eyes and fell asleep, dreaming of parents made of green goo.

CHAPTER 9

The Complications of Emotional Chemistry

The next morning Newton woke up first. He could hear Higgy snoring below him. Green bubbles floated up from the bottom bunk and popped when they hit the ceiling.

Newton did a quick check—still no memories before his arrival at Franken-Sci High—but he discovered that he was a little bit excited about the start of a new day. There was a tiny feeling growing inside him that maybe Franken Sci-High was exactly where he belonged.

He scurried out of the bunk, got dressed, and met up with Shelly in the hallway. They stopped off at his locker (the scanner tasted like blue cheese, which Newton liked, but not as much as he liked the kimchi) and grabbed smoothies in the cafeteria.

"The class schedule is different depending on the day of the week," Shelly explained as they slurped their smoothies. "On Tuesdays and Thursdays there's always

a chemistry lab for freshmen. You don't have one on your schedule yet, so you should come to lab with me and Theremin."

"Think he'll be in a better mood today?" Newton asked.

"I never know." Shelly sighed.

"How long does that thing last, where he can't do things well?"

"He calls it his 'low performance' stage," Shelly said. "Sometimes a few hours, sometimes days. It's unpredictable."

Newton drained his smoothie in one last slurp. "So what kind of chemistry class is this?" he asked.

"Quantum Emotional Chemistry for Nonemotional Chemistry Students," Shelly replied. "It's for beginners. I think you'll like Professor Snollygoster."

They reached the classroom, and Newton took a seat next to Shelly at a lab table. He noticed Mimi in the back row. She stared at him without saying hello. Odifin was there too, but it was hard to tell if the brain was staring at him or not.

Theremin floated in.

"Hello, Shelly," he said in a flat voice.

"Hey, Theremin," Shelly said, smiling.

"Are you feeling better, Theremin?" Newton asked.

"I'm sorry about the ketchup. I had no idea how dangerous it was for you."

But Theremin sat down on the other side of Shelly without a word.

At that moment Professor Snollygoster burst into the room. He had blue-black hair and violet-blue eyes, and wore a white lab coat over a white tie, shirt, and pants. He was also very tall, towering over the tallest kid in the class, who had telescoping legs.

"Good morning, class!" he said. "We've got an exciting experiment to work on today. Ah, I see a new face. You must be Newton."

Newton gave a little wave.

"Welcome to Quantum Emotional Chemistry for Nonemotional Chemistry Students," the professor said. "Do you have any questions?"

"Well, I guess it would be nice to know what emotional chemistry is," Newton said, and some of the students giggled. Theremin cracked a small smile.

"He should be in Quantum Emotional Chemistry for Non*thinking* Students," Odifin joked, and some more kids laughed.

Professor Snollygoster ignored Odifin. "Actually, it's a good question, Newton," he replied. "And the simple answer is that in this class we create chemical formulas

designed to effect human emotions."

Beep! A holographic image of Ms. Mumtaz's head materialized beside Snollygoster.

"Good morning, everyone! It's my pleasure to announce the first-place prize for this year's Mad Science Fair," the headmistress said. "Hold on to your lab coats . . . all members of the first-place team will win a portal pass!"

Some of the kids groaned.

"I heard those groans," she said. "But this year's prize is not just any ordinary portal pass. This portal pass will take you anywhere your heart desires, as long as it's on Earth and not endangering yourself or others."

Now the kids were whispering excitedly.

"So students—may the best project win!" Mumtaz said as her image dissolved away.

Anywhere your heart desires, Newton thought. *That was too good to be true!*

Newton looked at Shelly, his eyes wide.

"Did you hear that?" he whispered. "If the portal will take me anywhere, I can ask it to take me home, even though I don't have my parents' permission, and then I'll find out who I really am! Shelly, we have to win that prize!"

"There is no we," Theremin said. "Because Shelly and I

have not agreed to let you help us with our project."

"Theremin, what's the big deal?" Shelly asked.

"It's okay," Newton said quickly. "I'll just . . . I'll think of a project on my own."

"Good luck with that," Theremin hissed. "Have you ever done a science project before? Or is that something else you've forgotten?"

Newton winced.

"Theremin, that's not fair," Shelly said. "It's not Newton's fault that he can't remember anything from

before he came here. Have a heart."

"I do. I have *two* of them," Theremin whined. "The one Father put in my chest, and the spare in my locker!"

Professor Snollygoster cleared his throat loudly. "I think it's going to be a wonderful Mad Science Fair this year!" he said, clapping his hands together. "I will be happy to help any of you by reviewing your projects or lending you supplies. See me after class. And now, let's begin today's experiment. Shelly, can you partner with our new student for this, please?"

"Sure," Shelly said, with an annoyed glance at Theremin.

The robot rolled his eyes. "Fine."

Snollygoster held up a bottle with a red liquid inside it. "This is distilled *Metum Vitae*, in other words, Fear Serum. In its current state, it can make anyone exposed to it afraid of anything. For today's experiment, I want you to tweak the serum so that it only makes the subject afraid of harmless things. A baby bunny, for example, or a lollipop."

A murmur went up among the students. This was going to be a tough assignment.

"I've uploaded the revised formula to your tablets. You have thirty minutes. Begin!" the professor announced.

Newton glanced over at Theremin. Everybody else had a lab partner, but Theremin was working by himself. Newton felt a pang of sympathy for the robot.

"Maybe Theremin can work with us?" Newton asked Shelly.

"Let's let him cool off," Shelly whispered. "He's being ridiculous right now."

She started measuring liquid into a beaker. Newton kept looking at Theremin. The robot was mumbling to himself.

"Two milligrams . . . heat . . . agitate . . ."

He put his beaker over the flame of a Bunsen burner. *Poof!* A small explosion in the beaker resulted in a cloud of gray smoke.

"Better luck next time, Theremin," Snollygoster said. He held up Shelly and Newton's beaker. The previously red formula was now a deep purple color. "This looks perfect!"

Shelly and Newton high-fived each other. Theremin growled and crushed the glass beaker in his robot hand.

"Since you two are done early, perhaps you'd like to do an extra-credit assignment," Snollygoster suggested. "How else can you chemically modify the fear formula?"

Then he looked directly at Newton and said, "Just

use your old noodle noggin."

Noodle noggin. Newton's eye twitched as he heard the phrase. Ideas started churning in his brain.

"The potency of the base formula could be adjusted to control the level of fear experienced by the subject," Newton replied. "Or the formula could be reversed to cause the subject to feel courage. Or made more specific so that the subject could fear one particular person."

Newton didn't know how he knew this or where the thoughts were coming from. They were racing at him from all directions. He started rattling off dozens of complicated chemical formulas. When he finished, he opened his eyes and noticed the other students—even Shelly—staring open-mouthed at him. Snollygoster was grinning widely.

"Excellent, Newton!" he said. "I think perhaps this class is wasted on you. You should probably move into my Advanced Emotional Chemistry class."

"Really? Wow!" Newton said.

That was the last straw for Theremin. His own internal emotional chemistry boiled over. His eyes turned bright green.

"Aaaaaaargh!" With a frustrated yell, the robot angrily upended the lab table. Glass beakers shattered, liquids spilled on the floor and mixed together.

"Theremin, control yourself!" Snollygoster yelled as he ran to his desk and pressed a button. A small robotic vacuum rolled out from under his desk and began to suck up the chemical concoctions on the floor.

"Control?! I CAN'T!" Theremin yelled as he tossed aside his lab stool. It bounced across the floor and banged into Shelly's leg.

Newton stood up. "Theremin, cool it!"

"Shut up, Newton! You're not the boss of me!" Theremin cried, and he grabbed a roll of paper towels from another table and rapidly hurled them at Newton.

Newton easily ducked out of the way. "I'm not trying to boss you around, I'm trying to stop you!" he shot back. He lowered his head and ran to tackle Theremin.

By now, kids in the class were taking sides.

"Go, Theremin!"

"Go, new kid!"

The robot's levitating jets roared to life and Theremin shot straight up, avoiding the tackle. But Newton had too much momentum and banged into another lab table, knocking it down. The two students sitting at the table shrieked as they fell off their stools.

"Boys! Boys! Enough of this!" Snollygoster yelled.

Theremin floated over to a shelf and picked up a jar of rainbow-colored liquid.

Smash! He threw it on the ground and it shattered. Colorful confetti started raining down from the ceiling. The students who were hit by the confetti began laughing.

"Thank goodness that was just a Happiness formula," Snollygoster said, "but Theremin, you must stop this right now! Some of those chemicals are very dangerous!"

When Theremin looked over at Snollygoster, Newton leaped forward and grabbed the robot's legs, yanking him down to the ground in a wrestling hold.

"Give it up, Theremin!" Newton urged him.

"Please, Theremin, listen to Newton!" Shelly yelled.

"I. WILL. NOT. LISTEN. TO. YOUR. NEW. BEST. FRIEND!" Theremin yelled.

The robot broke out of Newton's grasp with a mighty surge of strength. He grabbed a test tube off the shelf, uncorked it, and threw the liquid at Newton.

Newton's body tingled as the concoction absorbed into his skin. Professor Snollygoster came running over and took the test tube from Theremin's hand so he could look at the label.

"Summer of Love," he said. "Fairly harmless."

"That's disappointing." Theremin sighed.

Newton shook his head and suddenly felt confused. If he had been a cartoon character, Newton's eyes would have formed into the shape of hearts. He lifted his head—and saw Mimi staring at him.

"Mimi!" he cried. "I love you!"

In the back of his mind, Newton heard laughing. But that didn't matter. All he knew was that he loved Mimi, and he didn't care who knew it!

"What are you talking about?" Mimi asked.

"It's . . . I can't explain it . . . my heart is aching . . . you're the only one for me," Newton said, and the other kids laughed again.

"It's the Summer of Love formula, Mimi," Shelly told her. "It's not real."

"Yeah, right," Mimi said, and her eyes narrowed suspiciously. Newton thought they were the most beautiful eyes he had ever seen.

"Theremin! Newton!" Professor Snollygoster yelled. "Come with me to Ms. Mumtaz's office right now!"

CHAPTER 10

Newton Lends a Hand

Professor Snollygoster grabbed each boy by the arm.

On the way out the door, Newton looked back at the rest of the class. "Oh no! I forgot to tell you that I love you!" he yelled with a dopey grin on his face. "I love you all!"

As the formula began to take maximum effect, Newton was overcome by a feeling of love for everyone he saw.

"And I love you too, Theremin," Newton said as Snollygoster dragged them down the hall. "You too, Professor Snollygoster."

"Oh dear," the professor said. "I really must adjust that formula. It's far too strong."

As they passed the school greenhouse, a bionic parrot flew overhead.

"Hello!" the parrot cawed.

"Yes, yes, hello!" Newton replied. "I love you!"

The parrot didn't miss a beat. "Love you too! Love you too!" It whistled.

Moments later they reached Mumtaz's office, and Snollygoster burst in without knocking. Mumtaz looked up from her desk and raised her eyebrows.

"These two rapscallions got into quite a scuffle," Snollygoster said. "I remit them into your capable hands now. I've got a classroom to clean up."

"Mobius Mumtaz?" Newton said, and then blurted out "I-love-you!" so fast it sounded like one word.

The headmistress glanced at Snollygoster and sniffed the air. "Summer of Love?"

"Theremin tossed a tube of it at Newton," Snollygoster reported, "and it seems to have absorbed into his skin quite quickly."

"Go clean up your classroom, Snolly," Mumtaz said. "I'll take care of this."

"Thank you," Snollygoster said, and quickly departed.

Mumtaz stood up and studied the two boys, then took a different tone. "I get it, Theremin. You and Shelly are close friends, and I'm guessing Newton here is coming between you. But you've got to learn to control your anger."

Theremin stared at the floor. Newton looked even more lovestruck than before.

"What you need is to get to know Newton better, Theremin," she said. "So you're going to eat lunch with Newton every day for a whole week and help him pass his portal test. If he doesn't pass, I'll fail you, too."

"But that's not fair!" Theremin whined.

"Trust me on this," Mumtaz said. "It's for the best. Now you two, go chill out in the garden until the Summer of Love formula wears off."

They followed orders and sat down on a bench. Theremin was silent, glaring straight ahead.

Newton found that he couldn't stop talking.

"I love this bench," he said. Then he touched the wall behind him. "And this wall. I love this whole place!"

"Sure you do," Theremin grumbled. "Why wouldn't you? Everyone thinks you're smart and awesome."

"I love that they think that!" Newton said cheerfully, and Theremin scowled.

They sat in silence for a long time. Then the bionic parrot flew over to them.

"Love you too! Love you too!" it said, perching on Newton's knee.

"I love—wait," Newton paused, scrunching up his eyes. "What am I saying? I don't love you. I mean, I'm sure you're a nice bird, but I don't really know you."

"Hey, I think the formula wore off," Theremin said.

Newton looked puzzled. "What formula?"

"The one I sort of, kind of, accidentally-on-purpose spilled on you," Theremin said. "Sorry. But it looks like you're fine now."

Theremin rose from the seat and started to float away.

"Um, Theremin? I do remember what Ms. Mumtaz said," Newton called after him. "Aren't we supposed to eat lunch together?"

Theremin stopped. "Oh yeah. Right," he said, in a voice that clearly said he wasn't thrilled with the idea. "We should stop at our lockers first and get books for our afternoon classes."

"Okay, sure," Newton said, relieved that Theremin

was being sort of nice for a change.

"So, um, I told a lot of people that I loved them, huh?" Newton said.

"Yes," Theremin said matter-of-factly. "Mimi, me, Professor Snollygoster . . ."

"Oh no!" Newton groaned. "Shelly too?"

Theremin thought about it. "No, not Shelly. Why? Do you like her?"

"Not like that," Newton said quickly. "She's just a friend. What about you?"

"She's my friend," Theremin said. "My *best* friend. And I get that you're friends with her now too, but I still don't want you to work with us on the science fair project, got it? I'll do what Ms. Mumtaz ordered, but that's it."

"I understand," Newton said. "Listen, I don't want to ruin your friendship with Shelly. I'll stop hanging out with her if you want."

"Yeah, well, that's the best idea you've had all day," Theremin said.

Newton reached his locker and sighed. He would miss being friends with Shelly. But Theremin was friends with her first. It was only fair. *This must be how the world works,* he thought.

Newton licked the locker pad—today it tasted like a

hamster—and opened the door. Then he gasped.

A hologram materialized in the middle of his locker! It looked just like an envelope.

"Touch your finger to the seal," Theremin instructed. "The envelope will open, and whoever sent it will know that you opened it."

Curious, Newton obeyed. A message popped up.

NEWTON:

PLEASE HAVE DINNER WITH ME TONIGHT AT AIRY CAFÉ. 7:00 SHARP.

MIMI CROWNINSHIELD

There was a circle with the word "yes" inside it, and one with the word "no."

"Where is the Airy Café?" Newton asked Theremin.

"Outside, near the dorms," Theremin replied. "Why? Are you thinking of going?"

Newton pressed yes. "Why not? I mean, it's not like I can eat with you and Shelly anymore."

Theremin's eyes flashed dark blue. He didn't say anything for a few seconds.

"I'm sure you'll have fun with Mimi," Theremin said finally, then floated over to his locker. Because he didn't have a tongue, or human eyes, or fingerprints, his locker had an old-school combination lock on it with an added security feature. A new combination was uploaded to his brain every day, and he spun the dial with his eye lasers.

Seventeen . . . twenty-four . . . six . . .

"Aaaaaaah!"

For a second, Newton thought that maybe Theremin had been surprised by a hologram invitation too. But then he realized that an intense, powerful force was sucking Theremin inside his locker!

Shelly's words about black holes from the day before popped into his head.

They'll suck you into—oblivion . . .

"Theremin!" Newton yelled. He rushed over and grabbed the robot's stubby legs as they almost disappeared inside his locker.

"Heeeeelp!" Theremin cried. Then the swirling force of the black hole caused his head to pop right off! Theremin quickly extended his arms, activating their telescoping feature, and grabbed his own head with his hands.

Meanwhile, Newton felt the floor shaking under his feet. The metal lockers up and down the hall clanked as they shook and rattled. Newton could feel his hair whip around his face as the force of the black hole began to pull at him as well.

Overhead, ceiling tiles vibrated, broke off, and

whizzed past Theremin, disappearing into the black hole. Then a metal garbage can came out of nowhere, crumpled, and got sucked in, followed by the Lost and Found box . . .

"Hang on, Theremin, I've got you!" Newton yelled.

With a loud grunt, Newton pulled on Theremin as hard as he could. He and the robot fell backward. Newton tossed Theremin aside, jumped up, and slammed the locker door shut. Then he spun the dial on the combination lock. Instantly, text books and equipment from the nearby Nano Technology Lab that had been hurtling down the hall clattered to the ground.

Exhausted, Newton sank to the floor. Theremin screwed his head back onto his body and floated over to him.

"Newton, why didn't you just let me get sucked into that black hole and step in as Shelly's best friend, after the way I've treated you? It doesn't make sense," Theremin said, flabbergasted. "Instead, you, you— saved me! You risked getting sucked in with me!"

Newton shrugged. "I might not remember much, but somehow, I know there's a difference between right and wrong," he said. "And I knew that saving you was the right thing to do."

Theremin paused.

"Newton, I'm so sorry," Theremin said, finally. "I acted horribly! I think you and I can both be friends with Shelly." The robot paused. "And maybe you and I can be friends too. What do you say?"

He held out a hand and helped Newton off the floor.

"Thanks," Newton said. "I'd like that."

"Let's go have lunch," Theremin said, and together, the two boys made their way to the cafeteria.

CHAPTER 11

Bubbly Burgers and Funny Fries

"Let me get this straight," Shelly said to Theremin a short while later as they ate lunch with Newton. "Not only are you cool with Newton being our friend, but you want him to work on the Mad Science Fair project with us, after all that?"

"That's right," Theremin said.

"Are you sure some of that love formula didn't get into your processors?" Shelly asked.

"Not a drop," Theremin said. "Chill, Shelly. Newton and I worked it out."

Shelly looked over at Newton, who nodded, adding, "We're buds."

"Well, I'm confused, but of course I want us all to work together. Partly because you're my friends," Shelly said, "and partly because it might give Newton more of a chance of winning that portal pass, finding his family, and finding out who he really is."

"True." Theremin smiled.

"That's what I'm counting on," Newton said. "So, what kind of projects are you thinking of?"

Shelly and Theremin looked at each other.

"Well, actually, we haven't thought of anything yet," Shelly admitted. "I mean, we've thought of *a lot* of things, but none of them were great ideas."

"She didn't like my hot ice cream idea," Theremin protested.

"I liked it in theory, but it sounds maddeningly impossible to make or enjoy as a dessert," Shelly countered. "But now that the three of us are a team, we can come up with something awesome. How about we brainstorm at dinner tonight?"

"To victory!" Theremin said as he pumped his fist in the air. "Group hug!"

Newton held back. "Um, I can't make it tonight," Newton said. "I'm having dinner with Mimi."

"Oh yeah, right," Theremin said as he settled to the floor.

"You're *what*?" Shelly's eyes got wide. "Okay, for a really weird day, that's the weirdest thing I've heard."

"She sent him a holo-invite," Theremin explained. "And I . . . I sort of lied and told him it would be fun. But that was before he saved my life and we bonded."

Shelly looked at Newton. "Just be careful around that girl. I'm not sure what she's up to, but it's usually not good."

"We could go to the library after dinner and do some research," Theremin suggested.

Newton nodded. "I'd like that."

Shelly held out her right arm. "Go team! Let's do this!"

Theremin rose off the floor and put his hand over Shelly's hand. Newton got the drift and put his hand over Theremin's. Then the three friends raised their arms in the air with a cheer.

"To victory!!"

That night Newton stepped out of the dorm building and followed the sign that read: AIRY CAFÉ THIS WAY. It wasn't a far walk through the jungle, but he heard strange chirps and shrill birdcalls and was happy to see the Airy Café up ahead. It was a tall, circular building made of frosted glass, and Mimi was already outside waiting for him. She tapped her fingernails, painted with her signature green nail polish.

"You're seventeen seconds late," she told him.

"Sorry, Mimi," he said.

She sighed. "Come on, let's go in."

Mimi pushed open the door and Newton followed her inside. She made a beeline for the hostess, a woman in a pale blue suit with a matching cap.

"Reservation for two. Crowninshield," Mimi said.

The woman smiled. "Of course, Mimi," she said. She waved her hand. "Please take your seats."

Two silver chairs slid up on a conveyor belt on the ground. Mimi sat in one, and Newton took her cue and sat in the other.

Suddenly, the chairs started to rise up, supported by poles. A port in the ceiling slid open, and Newton saw Mimi's hair begin to float in the air as they entered an

antigravity dining room. Then the chairs they were sitting on detached from the poles and continued to float straight up until they finally settled on either side of a round table!

"We're flying!" Newton cried.

"Not flying, *weightless*," Mimi explained. "Everything floats without gravity!"

Newton looked around and saw other diners sitting on tilting chairs around floating tables that were all askew. Everyone was laughing.

A server in a pale blue uniform floated over to their table.

"Hi, there," she said. "I'm Avi, your server. Have you been to the Airy Café before?" Then she burst into giggles.

"He hasn't, but I have, of course," Mimi said. "We'll take two Bouncy Burgers, two Funny Fries, and two Bubble Shakes, please."

Avi laughed. "Yes, of course!"

Then she floated away.

"Why was she laughing?" Newton asked.

"It's the weightlessness. It makes you feel silly after a while," Mimi responded. Then she leaned forward across the table. "Listen, Newton, that was a nice try today, pretending that you were in love with me to get information."

"I wasn't pretending," Newton said, and then he blushed. "I mean, I really felt it at the time, but it was only because of the formula Theremin spilled on me."

"So the robot's in on it too?" Mimi asked.

"In? In on what?" Newton asked.

"Your plan to get close to me and steal my science fair project idea, for starters," Mimi said. "I've been onto you from day one. But as my dad taught me, keep your friends close, and enemy spies closer. So here we are."

"Um, yes, here we are," Newton repeated. Mimi was making him feel like . . . like a bug under a microscope.

"So I have a proposition for you," she said. "You can hang out with me—instead of with that sniveling tin can and that animal-loving Goody Two-Shoes that you hang out with now."

Newton frowned. "But . . . they're my friends. And Theremin's not a tin can."

"They might be your friends, but they are at zero-point-zero on the social scale," Mimi said. "If you hang out with me, you'll be popular. And popular kids are the only ones that get ahead at Franken-Sci High."

Newton pondered this. Higgy didn't like Franken-Sci High much, and it was because a lot of students didn't want to hang out with him. And Theremin was angry all the time for the same reason. So maybe Mimi had a point. But was being popular worth giving up Theremin and Shelly?

Mimi leaned in even farther. "So if we're going to be friends, Newton, I need to know more about you. Where are you from?"

"I don't know," Newton replied.

"Come on, Newton, you can drop the act," Mimi said, smiling sweetly. "We're friends."

"I would tell you if I knew," Newton said sincerely. "But I don't. I don't have any memory of who I am or where I'm from."

"Are you saying you really have amnesia?" She blinked.

Newton shrugged. "Maybe. I don't remember."

"Order up!" Avi appeared next to them, smiling. She plopped their food down on the table.

Mimi quickly grabbed her plate and Newton did the same. "The plates and food will float away if you're not quick enough, Newton. We'd better eat."

Newton looked down at his burger. It was slowly separating, with toppings floating off in different directions. He grabbed the pieces, held them together, and took a bite. Then he put the burger down for a second, and it started to bounce away! He grabbed it and took another bite.

"Wow, they make you work for your food here,"

Newton said. "But it's kind of fun!"

Mimi smiled. "Try a fry."

Newton bit into a fry that had already floated up by his face.

Oo-ee! Oo-ee! A siren sound wailed.

"No way!" Newton said.

"Each one makes a different sound," Mimi explained. She bit into a fry, and hers let out a *tweet*.

Newton bit into another one.

Pfffffffft.

Newton blushed. "Oh man. That sounded like Higgy."

Mimi giggled. "Yes, that's a fart fry!"

Then Newton noticed that bubbles were floating out of his milkshake glass.

"You've got to catch them. Quickly!" Mimi said, showing him how it was done. "They turn into milkshakes once they hit your tongue."

Newton obeyed, catching the closest bubble by opening his mouth and letting the bubble float inside. It dissolved in his mouth with a creamy, sweet taste.

"Mmm, that's good!" Newton said. He floated up a little bit out of his chair to catch another bubble that was floating away. "Got it!"

Mimi laughed, and the two of them launched into a giggling fit.

Suddenly, the lights flickered. Newton's stomach dropped as his chair began to drop as well.

"Power surge!" someone yelled.

Instinctively, Newton reached for a nearby glass wall with his hands and feet, and clung to it as the lights flickered again.

A soothing voice came over a loudspeaker.

"Our antigrav system had a slight hiccup, but its working fine now. Please enjoy your meals."

Newton looked down. It was only when he saw that everyone was still floating safely, seated at their tables, that he realized he had done something strange. He had just overreacted, he realized, and he floated back into his seat.

Mimi was staring at him, her eyes wide.

"So uh, the system failed for a second there, right?" Newton asked, hoping to explain away what she just saw. "Antigravity works in mysterious ways?"

"I suppose." Mimi sighed, and then her eyes hardened and narrowed. "I'm really glad we did this, Newton, but its decision time. Friends?"

"Um, yeah, sure," Newton said, "but I still want to be friends with Theremin and Shelly, too."

Mimi scowled and her voice went cold. "Sorry, Newton. No deal. Either you're with me—or you're against me."

Even the fun of the Airy Café couldn't lighten Mimi's mood after that. Newton wondered why she was so suspicious of him.

Why would she think I'm a spy? he wondered. But then it hit him—why wouldn't she? *I appeared out of nowhere and I don't even know who I am.*

Now Newton's eyes narrowed, but not with suspicion—with determination.

Shelly, Theremin, and I are going to win that Mad Science Fair prize, no matter what it takes! he promised himself. *It's the only way I can find out who I really am!*

Eureka!

"Ha ha. A fart fry. That is funny," Theremin said the next morning, when he and Shelly joined Newton for breakfast smoothies.

Theremin didn't need to eat, of course, but he wanted to hear about Newton's dinner with Mimi.

"I've never been to the Airy Café," Shelly admitted. "I'm a little afraid of heights."

"It was kinda fun," Newton said.

"And Mimi was really mean to you, right?" Theremin asked.

Newton shook his head. "No, actually, she was pretty nice. She did ask me a lot of questions, though, and it got me thinking. We really need to win the science fair, so I can get some answers."

"I'm sure we'll come up with something great tonight," Shelly assured him.

"Why wait? Can we meet right after classes are

over?" Newton asked. "I really want to get on it."

"Sure, why not?" Shelly replied. "First, though, you have to finalize your schedule."

"Oh yeah, right," Newton said. He took out his tablet, scrolled to the enrollment screen, and selected his classes. The good news was that Leviathan was teaching Neo Evolutionary Biology. The bad news? Juvinall was the only gym teacher who had an opening in her class, and Physics of Physical Education was a requirement.

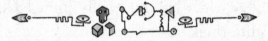

Newton spent the rest of the day half-focused on his classes and half-focused on trying to think of ideas for the science fair project. He wasn't the only one who was obsessed. It was all the students were talking about, though Newton noticed that some bragged loudly about their projects, while others talked in whispers.

In the hallways, kids were rushing around gathering equipment for their projects. He spotted Tootie controlling an antigravity platform that suspended a big, bulky box in the air. The box had small holes in the sides, and Newton swore he heard scratching sounds. When he asked Tootie what was inside, she just smiled and said, "Something terrifyingly awesome!" He wasn't sure he wanted to know!

After his last class, Newton met Shelly and Theremin outside the library. He stared up at the glass walls of the Brain Bank.

"I can't believe it's only been a few days since I first met you guys in there," he said.

Shelly nodded. "I know! So much has happened."

"So, let's download ideas from the brains!" Newton suggested.

"Against the rules," Shelly replied. "We're supposed to come up with ideas on our own."

"Besides the Brain Bank, the library has some paper books, like Professor Waggs likes," Theremin explained. "And then, there are the holo-books."

The robot drifted over to a glass pedestal with a square platform on top and waved his hand over it. A holographic image of a book appeared. Theremin waved his hand again, and, as the holo-pages turned, three-dimensional images and diagrams popped out.

"Whoa!" Newton exclaimed. "Cool."

They found a quiet table in the back of the library.

"So I was thinking," Shelly said, "that maybe we could expand on the rodent-protection system I've been developing."

"Rodent protection?" Newton asked.

Shelly reached under her poncho and gently pulled

out a white rat with a pink nose and a long, pink tail.

"Cats give these little guys such a hard time," she said. "I was thinking of inventing a sonic collar that would repel them."

"Hmm," said Theremin thoughtfully. "Wouldn't it bother the rats, too?"

"Exactly my problem," Shelly admitted. "I need to read up more on buffering sonic technology. Let me go find some books."

With that, she headed off.

"Now what do we do?" Newton asked.

"I've been thinking," Theremin said. "Mumtaz wants me to help you practice for your portal test. If we win the contest and you don't know how to access the portal, it won't be of much use to you. We'd better practice."

"Good point. Whoever said you weren't a smart robot?" Newton said as he dug the brochure out of his bag.

"Thanks. Fold the corners of the brochure in first," Theremin instructed.

Determined to get it right, Newton carefully folded down one corner. Then he tried to fold another—and, just as before, his fingers stuck to the brochure.

"That should not be happening," Theremin remarked.

"EXACTLY, it shouldn't!" Newton yelled out, a little too loudly. A drone instantly appeared, floated up to him, and a message flashed across its digital screen.

SSSSHHHHHH!

"Sorry," Newton told the drone, and it flew away. Newton lowered his head and focused on folding the brochure again. Sweat was dripping down his face. As he got his fingers unstuck, they just kept sticking again.

"Let me see that," Theremin said, and he grabbed the brochure from Newton as Shelly walked up, carrying an armful of books and a holo-book.

"Hey, good idea to—" Shelly stopped and looked at Newton. Her mouth dropped open. "Newton, are you all right? Your eyes are all—"

"I'm never going to fold my brochure correctly!" Newton blurted loudly, frustrated. "It won't matter if we win the science fair or not if I can't open the portal!"

The drone returned and flashed the warning:

I SAID . . . SHHHH!

"Sorry," Newton said, then he scowled. "No, I'm not sorry! It's been days and I still don't know who I am! Mumtaz seems to know something, but she won't tell me anything! And my only chance of finding out what is going on is winning the contest, and I can't even fold a dumb piece of paper. It's not fair!"

Multiple red lights began flashing on the drone.

EJECTED! EJECTED! LEAVE NOW!!

Five more drones swooped in and surrounded Newton. They started to herd him out of the library.

"Newton!" Shelly called after him.

Newton didn't answer. He left the library and headed back to the dorm.

There's no point in me winning the science fair, he thought gloomily. *No point in anything, really.*

When he got to his room, he didn't even check for any of Higgy's pranks before he opened the door and stepped inside. Luckily, Higgy hadn't set one.

"Where've you been, roomie?" Higgy asked.

"Wasting my time," Newton mumbled. He kicked off his shoes and scurried up to the top bunk.

Higgy got up from his chair. He was wrapped in a bathrobe, but his face was bandaged, and he wore his usual cap and glasses. "Okay, Newton, you have to tell me what your secret is," he said.

"What secret?" Newton asked. "I told you, I don't know who I am or where I'm from."

"No, I mean the secret of how you get in the top bunk," Higgy said. "You climb up there so fast. And you don't use the ladder."

"What do you mean?"

Higgy walked over to the metal ladder on the front of the bunk and tapped it with a gooey tendril. "I can just

slither up the rail if I want. And other humans climb, like this," Higgy demonstrated. "But that's not what you do. You kind of . . . scurry your body up the rail and barely touch the rungs. So what's your secret?"

"Honestly, I don't know," Newton said. "I thought I was doing it, you know, the normal 'human' way."

"All we need is a little scientific deduction," Higgy said. "Do it again."

Curious, Newton jumped down from the top bunk and then scurried up the ladder again.

"Hmm," said Higgy. "It's like the palms of your hands stick to the metal, so you don't need to grip the ladder rungs or step on them. We could use a microscope about now. Message your friend Theremin."

"How do I do that?" Newton asked.

"With your tablet," Higgy replied. "I'll show you."

Newton gave Higgy his tablet, and one of Higgy's green tentacles snaked out and scrolled through the screen.

"Students . . . freshmen . . . there he is, Theremin Rozika," Higgy said, handing the tablet back to Newton. "Now type in a message telling him to come here."

"Okay," Newton replied, happy to play along if it meant finding out answers about himself.

A few minutes later there was a knock on the door. Newton opened it, and Theremin and Shelly stepped in.

"Newton, are you okay?" Shelly asked. "We really need to talk to you about something."

"First, we need Theremin's microscope, please," Higgy said. "I've deduced that Newton has an unusual stickiness to his fingertips, and perhaps also his toes."

Shelly and Theremin exchanged knowing looks, and then a door opened on Theremin's chest and a small retractable microscope came out.

"Okay, Newton. Put your finger under the lens," Theremin instructed.

Newton obeyed. Higgy looked through the lens first. "Yes, yes. His digits seem a bit unusual, but I can't quite figure out what I'm looking at."

Then Shelly looked—and gasped.

"Your fingers seem to be equipped with tiny hairlike structures, Newton," Shelly said. "It's similar to . . . to the setae of wall-climbing reptiles."

"I can cling to walls," Newton said. "I've done it."

"That's because your finger pads are super grippy," Theremin said. "That's probably why you haven't been able to fold the brochure to get the portal. Your fingers stick to it."

"Reptiles can control when they grip and when they don't," Shelly explained, her voice rising with excitement. "Your body may have activated this reptilian function

under stress. You could always wear gloves when you take the portal test. That would solve the problem."

"Right!" Newton said. It felt good to have an answer—well, sort of an answer. A bunch of other questions flooded his mind.

"Could this be a clue?" he asked. "Maybe I'm from a family of mad scientists with grippy fingertips?"

Shelly and Theremin looked at each other again.

"Um, I'm not sure," Shelly said. "Listen, Newton, the stuff we wanted to talk to you about—your grippy fingers are part of it, I think."

She took out her tablet. "I've been taking notes the last few days, to try to help figure out what your deal is," she said. "I don't have all the answers yet, but I should tell you what I've observed."

"You've noticed stuff about me?" Newton asked.

Shelly nodded. "Remember when we snuck into Mumtaz's office, and she walked in on us? You flattened yourself against the wall. I saw you from the closet. You sort of just . . . blended in."

"Really?" Newton asked. "So that's why she couldn't see me."

"Also, you can see in the dark. And when you jumped in the pool, you sort of blended in with the water and the blue tiles on the floor," Shelly added.

"And that's not all. Newton, when you came out of the pool I could swear I saw . . . *gills* on your neck."

"Like a fish?" Higgy asked. "Cool!"

"Like a fish, or maybe . . . maybe an amphibian," Shelly said.

Newton looked down at his hands. "Super-grippy fingertips."

"And toes, too, I'll bet," Higgy said.

"Does all that mean . . . ?" Newton asked. "That I'm not human?"

Shelly shook her head. "I don't know. You sure look human. You're just . . . an extra-special one."

"I'll say!" Higgy exclaimed. "Those grippy fingers are pretty cool, roomie." He held up his goo hands. "I can bounce and slide down walls, but I'm not great at gripping anything. My gloves help a little, but it's nothing compared to your gripabilities. Hands like yours sure would come in handy."

Shelly laughed. "They sure would," she said. "But right now, we have to focus on an idea for our project. I don't think my sonic rat collar is going to come together in time."

"That's okay, Shelly. Next time," Theremin said.

Shelly went on. "I'll try to think of something else tonight," she said, "but maybe we can put our

noodle noggins together in the morning, as Professor Snollygoster says."

Newton twitched. He blinked. Then he cried out. "I have a great idea for our science fair project," Newton said, looking down at his hands. "A real *handy* idea, as a matter of fact."

Shelly grinned. "I like the way you're thinking, Newton. Do you think we can do it in time?"

Calculations and designs for his idea were rolling through Newton's brain.

"I'd say there's a 91.57638 percent chance that we can!" he replied.

"Count me in," said Theremin. "Whatever it is."

"Me too," Shelly said. Then she turned to Higgy. "Higgy, do you want to join us?"

Higgy shook his head. "No thanks. I'm already working on my project. But you guys go for it."

After making plans to meet up with Newton soon to get started, Shelly and Theremin left. Newton felt weary from the busy day, but filled with a new determination.

He, Shelly, and Theremin were going to make the greatest Mad Science Fair project ever and win the first-place prize, and all he needed to access the portal pass was a pair of gloves to fold the brochure!

We have to win! he thought as he drifted off to sleep.

CHAPTER 13

May the Best Mad Scientist Win!

In the days leading up to the Mad Science Fair, the students at Franken-Sci High got even more caught up in the frenzy and excitement.

They filled the library, talking and researching, until library drones started crash-landing. Their batteries had died from having to say "Shhhh!" so much.

They received packages in the mail that smoked and snorted and shook, containing ingredients for projects.

They prepared elaborate displays to show off their projects, filling the halls with the sounds of drills, hammers, liquids gurgling, and centrifuges spinning.

Newton, Shelly, and Theremin did most of their work in Newton's dorm room because they knew they could trust Higgy to keep their project a secret.

Even so, every time Newton bumped into Mimi in the halls, she would ask the same question.

"So, what project are you guys working on, Newton?

You can tell me. I'll keep it to myself."

But Newton, under strict orders from Shelly and Theremin, didn't share their plans with anyone.

It was a good thing, too, because as the science fair approached, strange things began to happen.

Odifin and Rotwang's experiment went missing, then turned up in the garbage. On the bright side, since it was about how to breed roses to smell stinkier than foot fungus, they were able to salvage it without much damage.

Then Tootie's antigravity platform was tampered with and began flinging her big box into the jungle instead of holding it in midair. But whatever was inside it was so loyal it came trotting back, shuffling along in the box until it reached her side again.

It seemed like every day experiments were being lost, damaged, or ruined.

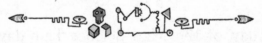

"It has to be Mimi, right?" Shelly whispered to Newton and Theremin at the school store one day when they were buying snacks.

"Seems likely," Theremin said.

But Newton wasn't so sure. "There are a lot of power-hungry students at this school, and any one of them

could be trying to sabotage the other contestants," he said. "Whoever it is, they aren't very good at it."

"Thank goodness for that," Shelly said. "Or that poor, defenseless lizard would have been toast when someone turned up the heat in its tank. How could anyone do that?"

That's when Newton thought he saw a flash of Mimi's hair behind a row of snack food. "Did you see that?" he asked Theremin and Shelly. "I think Mimi heard us."

"So?" Theremin said.

As awful as Mimi could be, Newton didn't want to hurt her feelings if she had overheard them. He knew that she wanted desperately to be brilliant at everything, even sabotage. Suddenly, he felt bad for her. Even so, he was happy to find out soon after that the sabotaging seemed to stop.

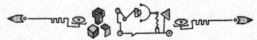

Soon, the day of the Mad Science Fair dawned and Newton awoke to the sound of pounding on his door.

Newton jumped out of bed and opened the door. Shelly raced in with Theremin floating behind her. She handed Newton a smoothie.

"I know it's early, but I'm so excited!" she said. "A lot of kids are already in the Hall of Mad Science, setting

up their projects and displays."

She motioned toward the bottom bunk. "Looks like Higgy's one of them."

Newton followed her gaze. "You're right! I must have been sleeping when he left. We should get going!"

Newton grabbed a cardboard box from his desk and they went outside, where a large wooden crate held their display. Theremin easily hoisted it above his head, and Newton's eyes widened.

"Superstrength," Theremin said. "One of the benefits of being a robot."

"So, the judging starts at ten," Shelly told Newton as they walked. "The teachers will judge the projects and vote for the best one. There's a prize for first, second, and third. But only the first-place winner gets the portal pass!"

Newton nodded. He wanted to win so badly that he could taste it.

When they arrived at the Hall of Mad Science, it was noisy with the sounds of students setting up their projects. Newton stopped when they stepped inside, taking it all in.

A large banner overhead read, WELCOME TO THE MAD SCIENCE FAIR!

Newton recognized some of the students.

Tootie Van der Flootin was walking around with a one-eyed, one-horned purple monster on a chain leash. It looked quite sweet at first glance, but when anyone but Tootie tried to pet it, the monster roared, displaying rows and rows of razor-sharp teeth.

Gustav Goddard's display had a curved sign that read: WHAT'S MORE FUN THAN BALLOON ANIMALS? SENTIENT BALLOON ANIMALS! Above him, a dog made of blue balloons was chasing a cat made of yellow balloons.

Tori Twitcher proudly stood in front of a glass aquarium with a robotic shark she had created swimming around inside it and snapping its jaws.

Newton couldn't believe all the great inventions and experiments. Everywhere he turned, he saw something new and inventive.

Edible tattoos.

Gravity in a can.

Elevator fart eraser spray.

Newton started to feel nervous. "These are some great projects."

"Ours is great too," Shelly assured him. "Look, here's our spot. D-17."

Theremin dropped the crate with a clatter and they quickly began to assemble their display. Newton's

confidence started to climb. Their invention was really a winner.

Mimi walked up just as they were putting on the finishing touches. She stopped and folded her arms across her chest.

"This is your winning invention?" she snorted. "A bookshelf?"

The center of the display featured a very tall metal bookshelf, as tall as the shelves in the library.

"No, Mimi, but nice try," Shelly said. "Newton, why don't you demonstrate?"

"Sure," Newton said. He slipped on their real invention—a pair of opalescent gloves and matching socks—and approached one of the slippery, flat sides of the bookcase. Then he casually climbed to the top shelf, using the gloves and socks to stick to the side. He took a book from the top shelf and climbed back down.

"We call them Sticky Savers," Shelly said proudly. "No ladders needed! No complicated gear! You can carry the gloves and socks in your backpack, so you can climb whenever you need to!"

Newton was grinning with pride from ear to ear. After all, the invention had been inspired by his own biology. He suddenly got worried that Mimi would remember when he hung on to the glass wall of the Airy Café during the power surge. Would she put two and two together and realize their invention was based on his strange ability?

Mimi's eyes narrowed. "Hmm," she said. "That's a pretty sophisticated invention created by somebody with *amnesia*."

Newton took a deep breath. She didn't seem to be onto him or realize he had special talents.

At that, Odifin rolled up, with Rotwang close behind. "If you even believe that he has amnesia. I don't believe it for a second," he said. "There's something not right about you, Newton Warp."

"Speaking of 'not right,'" Theremin noted, "you do realize you're a brain floating in a jar, don't you, Odifin?"

Mimi sniffed. "Well I have more brains than all of you combined, and you're not going to win this. *My*

invention is the best this school has ever seen!"

She stuck her nose in the air, turned, and walked away, as Odifin and Rotwang followed after her.

"What is her invention, anyway?" Shelly asked.

"Only one way to find out," Theremin said. "Come on! Follow me."

Shelly stayed behind to watch over their project while Theremin and Newton followed Mimi as she strolled down the crowded rows of displays. Then they froze when they heard farting sounds.

Pffft! Pffft! Pffft!

Higgy walked up behind them wearing shoes with thick, springy heels.

"Hey, guys!" he said. "Like my invention?"

"Fart Shoes?" Newton guessed.

"The first and only!" Higgy said, taking another step. *Pffft!* "They're a hit. Everyone's trying out my proto-type pairs."

Higgy was right. Farting sounds were sprouting up around them in all directions.

"Nice, Higgy!" Newton said. "Good luck!"

They spotted Mimi up ahead and followed her to the largest display in the room. It was a huge volcano that nearly touched the ceiling. A large bubble covered the top of the volcano.

Mimi noticed the two boys and grinned. "Jealous of my crowning achievement?"

"Looks more like a third-grade science project," Theremin said. "What's so great about an artificial volcano?"

"*This* is just the prototype." Mimi smiled as she rubbed her hands together. "The real ones will be life-size—and portable—working volcanoes! Just think about it: They're perfect for world domination! Some town doesn't want to give in to your demands? Just plop down one of these babies. Nothing inspires mad-scientist devotion like a volcano that can erupt at the touch of a button. My parents' company will probably even manufacture it. It's going to be huge."

"What's that bubble on top for?" Newton asked.

"For demonstration purposes only, Newton," Mimi replied. "So the volcano can erupt without melting down the place."

She pressed a button, and the volcano erupted. The bubble contained the lava, diverting it into a tank.

"Heatproof bubble, heatproof tank," Mimi said.

Newton had to admit that he was impressed. "Wow, Mimi," he said. "That's pretty awesome."

"Of course it is," Mimi responded.

Newton and Theremin walked back to their display.

"I don't know, Theremin," Newton said, worried. "There are a lot of amazing projects here, and Mimi's is, like, super amazing. I know she *thought* she was building a portable volcano, but that bubble tank idea could really save lives by protecting people from eruptions, whether she intended it to do that or not. I don't think we can win."

"Never say never!" Theremin said, and then he stopped in front of another display area where people were wearing goggles. "Ooh, cool," Theremin said, looking up at the sign. "It's Predictive Virtual Reality."

He pointed to a girl staring wide-eyed in front of them.

"What's that?" Newton asked.

Then the girl who made the goggles stepped up. "Well, regular virtual reality is technology that makes you feel like you're experiencing something, only you're really just seeing a video in real time," she said. "This is, like, one step better. It predicts the future of some of the science fair projects here. I recorded them and then applied a program that can illustrate what will most likely happen next." She removed the goggles. "Here, try them. Take a look at a display and then press the fast forward button to see how it'll turn out. Or press rewind to see what happened before."

"Got it!" Newton said.

He put the goggles on and looked at the next experiment—about using cafeteria food to make an all-in-one meal called hamburger cheesecake. He fast-forwarded, and could see the future of the experiment. The leftover hamburger cheesecake quickly grew mold, got thrown in a compost bin, was dumped into a garden, and a bunch of sunflowers grew from it.

"Cool!" Newton said. "Let me try another one."

The next display was an experiment to determine the ideal artificial environment to help lizards survive on Mars. This time, Newton stared through the goggles at a lizard perched on the glass wall of its tank, then pressed rewind.

As he watched, the lizard got smaller and smaller. Suddenly, the tank got brighter.

Soon he saw why: At what appeared to be nighttime because the image was dark, Newton could see a hand in the background turning up the dial on the heat lamp. It was wearing Mimi's green nail polish!

Shelly and Theremin had been right about Mimi sabotaging the experiments!

He almost took off the goggles then to tell Theremin, but he decided against it. He didn't want to get Mimi in trouble.

As he was thinking, the experiment kept rewinding, and the lizard got even smaller. It transformed into a tadpole, and then the tadpole became an egg.

Newton looked at it in wonder.

An egg . . .

Something flashed in Newton's brain, and it wasn't the Predictive Virtual Reality image.

It was what seemed to be a memory flooding back to him. He was inside a bubble . . . a pod, filled with water. He couldn't see through the pod; it was foggy. But then a bright light came on, and he could see shadows around the pod . . . people . . .

Sparks fell from the ceiling. The pod cracked open a bit . . . and . . .

The memory stopped. "Nooo!" Newton yelled. He stumbled around, trying to take off the goggles, but he couldn't. He felt a robot hand tear the goggles off his face.

"Are you okay?" Theremin asked.

Newton nodded, but he was panting and sweating. Kids were staring at him. He took a deep breath and tried to make it seem like nothing was wrong.

"I mean, nooo way! That was so cool!" he said weakly, still shaken.

That's when Higgy showed up and stepped in.

Pffft! Pffft! Pffft! "Hey everybody, check it out! Farty dancing!" Higgy yelled, and busted into dance moves. Everybody forgot about Newton's outburst and started laughing at Higgy.

Thanks, Newton mouthed to Higgy.

Newton and Theremin made their way back to their Sticky Savers display, and Newton tried to pull Shelly aside.

"What took you guys so long?" Shelly asked. "The judges were here already. I did the demonstration for them. They seemed to like it. But what happened?"

"We got distracted by some of the displays," Theremin replied. "Newton got rattled by something."

"Not rattled. I . . . I think I remembered something!" Newton said.

"Really?" Shelly asked eagerly. "What was it?"

But then they heard Mumtaz's voice.

"It's time to announce our winners!" she said from behind a lectern. "Please join us at the main stage."

Newton looked at his friends. "Well, this is it."

On a table beside Ms. Mumtaz, there were three trophies: a big one for first prize, a shorter one for second prize, and an even tinier one for third prize. The school's professors sat in chairs behind her, including Wagg, Juvinall, Leviathan, Phlegm, Snollygoster, and the others.

Professor Leviathan even caught Newton's eye and gave him a not-so-subtle thumbs up. He held his breath. Was she signaling that he and Shelly and Theremin were the winners?

"We'll start with third prize, which is a feast at Airy Café," Mumtaz announced. "I'm pleased to announce that it goes to a group of talented freshmen. Shelly Ravenholt, Theremin Rozika, and Newton Warp, for their Sticky Savers!"

Ms. Mumtaz held up the gloves and socks for all to see. Everyone cheered.

Newton tried to smile, but he was disappointed. There was only one prize that really mattered to him, and it wasn't that one.

Shelly squeezed his hand. "Sorry, Newton. We tried our best."

"Yeah, I know." Newton sighed. "At least we had a chance to work on something together. You, me, and Therem—"

Ruuuumble!

All of a sudden, the floor of the Science Hall began to shake. Displays began to topple over. Everyone turned to see smoke rushing out of Mimi's volcano. It was about to erupt.

"Miss Crowninshield, please turn that off!" Ms.

Mumtaz warned. "Mimi, now!"

Mimi was frantically pressing a button on her remote control device. "I'm trying! It's not working!"

The bubble above the volcano shattered and heat-proof glass hit the floor.

Mimi screamed. "Run for your lives! It's going to erupt lava . . . *real* lava!"

Then she yanked the gloves and socks out of Ms. Mumtaz's hands and slipped them on her own hands and feet.

As everyone scrambled toward the exits, Theremin picked up Newton and Shelly in each arm and lifted them off the floor to keep them safe from the flood of lava that might flow from the volcano at any second.

The volcano shuddered . . . and a small glop of lava shot from the top, slid down the side, . . . and stuck there. The ground stopped shaking, and everyone looked around in disbelief.

"Oh," said a voice, and everyone looked up. "That was all . . . on purpose!"

It was Mimi.

She had freaked out when she thought she was in danger and climbed up the wall of the Hall of Mad Science using the Sticky Savers. Now she was on the ceiling. When the students noticed her, many of them started laughing.

"Quiet, everyone," Ms. Mumtaz told them, and then looked up at Mimi. "Come down, please, Miss Crowninshield."

"No!" Mimi yelled. "It's not my fault. My volcano is perfect!" she tried.

Ms. Mumtaz sighed. "Mimi, it malfunctioned. It's

okay. But if you don't come down right this instant, it will be a mistake. I'm going to have to come get you," she threatened.

"You wouldn't!" Mimi dared her.

In a flash, Ms. Mumtaz put on another set of Sticky Savers and climbed up to the ceiling. Mimi scowled, knowing she had been defeated, and followed the head-mistress back down to the floor.

"Okay, everyone," Ms. Mumtaz called out. "The show's over. We all make mistakes sometimes."

Mimi just scowled. She threw the socks and gloves to the floor and stormed out.

That's when Professor Leviathan walked up to Ms. Mumtaz and tapped her on the shoulder. Then she whispered something in her ear.

"Settle down, everyone!" she called out. "There has been a change in the judging. Recent events have shown that the Sticky Savers have important applications in emergency situations. For that reason, the judges have decided to award Shelly, Theremin, and Newton first prize! Second prize goes to Tabitha Talos for her Predictive Virtual Reality goggles, and third prize goes to Gustav Goddard for Sentient Balloon Animals. Congratulations, everyone!"

Shelly and Theremin rushed onstage, but Newton

froze, stunned, as cheers erupted around him.

Tootie nudged Newton, and he walked onstage in a daze. Together, the three friends accepted their first-place trophy.

"You know what this means," Ms. Mumtaz said. "A special portal pass for each of you. Start thinking about where you want to go."

I already know, Newton thought, and then he realized something.

That memory that had come flooding back hadn't necessarily been a good one. He had been so eager to find answers, and now . . . well, he wasn't sure if he wanted them. Franken-Sci High was starting to feel like home, and it was a remarkable place to be.

"We did it, Newton!" Shelly said, hugging him. Theremin gave him a high-five.

Pffft! Pffft! Pffft! "Go, Newton!" Higgy cheered from the floor, doing a victory dance.

Newton smiled. *Whatever those answers are, I'm ready for them!* he thought. He knew he could handle anything, with the help of his friends.

Then he slipped on a pair of Higgy's farty shoes and started to dance.

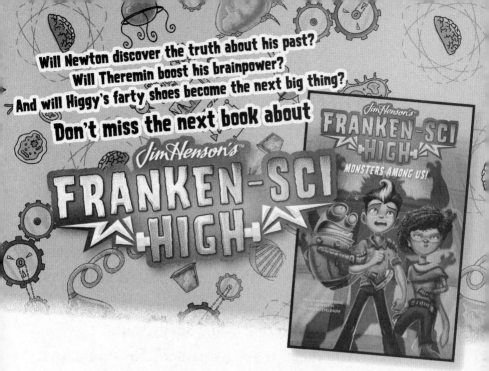

Will Newton discover the truth about his past?
Will Theremin boost his brainpower?
And will Higgy's farty shoes become the next big thing?
Don't miss the next book about

Jim Henson's™

FRANKEN-SCI HIGH

Jim Henson's
FRANKEN-SCI HIGH
MONSTERS AMONG US!

CREATED BY KATHY STIRTING
ILLUSTRATED BY
SHANAN PEPELBAUM

"*Ca-wee! Ca-wee! Ca-wee!*"

Newton Warp opened his eyes. In front of him, a
purple fuzzy monster with a snout like a trumpet was
hovering in the air, flapping its wings.

"*Ca-wee! Ca-wee! Ca-wee!*" The shrill, annoying
sound streamed out of the monster's snout.

"All right, all right, I'm awake," Newton mumbled.

He threw off his covers and jumped down off the top
bunk. The monster followed him, still tooting.

He ducked his head into his roommate's bottom
bunk.

"Higgy! There's a flying monster in here! Is this
supposed to be happening?" he asked.

The blob of green goo under the covers stirred, and two eyeballs peeked out.

"A monster? I would guess that your friend Shelly has something to do with that," Higgy replied. "Now, if you'll excuse me, I'm not ready to wake up yet." He rolled over.

Shelly, of course! Newton realized. He picked up the tablet on top of his dresser and tapped on Shelly's name.

A tiny hologram of Shelly's face appeared in front of him. She grinned.

"Oh good! Woller found you," Shelly said.

"Woller? You mean that's its name?" Newton asked, brushing the monster away from his face.

"He's my latest creation. He's one part butler and one part annoying alarm clock." Shelly said. "I sent him to wake you up. We've got that early morning meeting with Headmistress Mumtaz, remember?"

"How could I forget?" Newton asked. "You know how important this is to me."

"Well, hurry up and get ready," Shelly said. "We don't want to be late."

"Ca-wee! Ca-wee!"

"And do I get rid of Woller?" Newton asked.

"Just let him follow you," Shelly said, and then her face disappeared.

Newton sighed, grabbed a towel and a small bag, and headed to the bathroom down the hall in the dormitory. Still half-awake, he stopped in front of the mirror and yawned. Then he tasted peppermint.

Woller had stuck a toothbrush in Newton's mouth and was brushing Newton's teeth. When Newton stepped toward the sink to rinse out his mouth, Woller beat him to it and gave him a cup filled with water. Newton shrugged and decided to let the monster take care of him. It was almost like being asleep while someone else took care of the boring stuff. Woller turned on the shower and when the temperature was perfect, nudged Newton in. Then the shower's usual features took over. The walls were outfitted with lights that changed color according to the mood of the person showering. They quickly switched from a neutral silver to a peaceful, glowing blue, and relaxing music started to play. As two robot arms scrubbed Newton's hair, Newton started to feel more awake. The color of the shower turned to a cheerful yellow, and the music became more upbeat. When Newton started singing along, a robotic arm sprang out of the wall and shoved a waterproof karaoke microphone at him! Newton didn't really know the words, of course, so he didn't engage. He suddenly got a little sad.

So much had happened since that day, just a few weeks ago, that he'd woken up in Franken-Sci High. He had no memory—just a student ID card and a strange bar code on his foot. Luckily, he'd met Shelly Ravenholt and her friend Theremin Rozika, and they helped him get used to the strange school for mad scientists, although it had been a rocky start.

As a robot arm scrubbed his back, Newton thought back to his first days at Franken-Sci High. Theremin was an underachieving robotic student with an anger management problem. He'd been best friends with Shelly before Newton showed up on campus and had quickly become jealous of Newton and Shelly's fast friendship. Thanks to Headmistress Mumtaz's intervention, they'd worked things out. Then Shelly, Theremin, and Newton had worked on a project for the Science Fair—and won! The prize was a special portal pass that Newton hoped would help him find out who he really was and where he came from. . . .